Goodbye, Johnny Onions

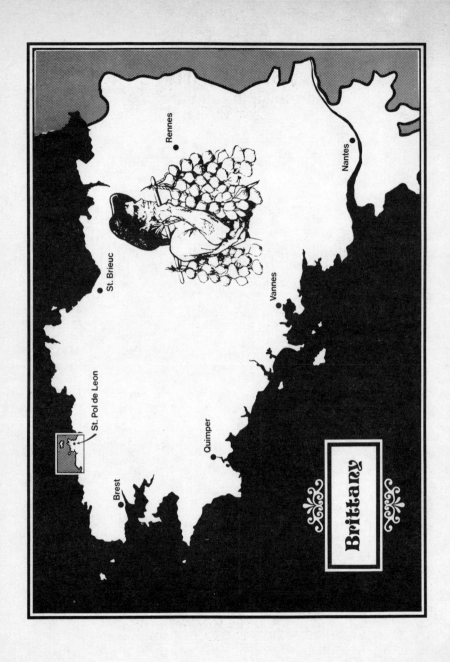

Rennes

Nantes

St. Brieuc

Vannes

St. Pol de Leon

Quimper

Brest

Brittany

Goodbye, Johnny Onions

Gwyn Griffiths

DYLLANSOW
TRURAN

First published 1987 by Dyllansow Truran, 'Trewolsta', Trewirgie, Redruth, Kernow.

© 1987 Gwyn Griffiths

ISBN 1 85022 031 X

Typeset by St. George Typesetting, Commercial Centre, Wilson Way,
Pool Industrial Estate, Redruth, Cornwall
Printed in Great Britain by A. Wheaton & Co. Ltd., Exeter

Acknowledgements

I owe a special word of thanks to my good friend Robert Simon, Plabennec, and his family for their assistance and kindness while compiling this book.

I am also greatly indebted to Steve Benbow, Claude Deridon and Peta Claude Corre (the last two, sadly, no longer with us) for a number of photographs:

to Mostyn Davies, Pontypridd, for the map;

to Madame Cecile Milin, Brest, for invaluable assistance in tracking down the two ballads on the disaster of the "Hilda";

to Mrs Elinor Beynon for typing the manuscript.

Finally, to Dyllansow Truran my heart-felt gratitude for their interest and enthusiasm in publishing this little volume.

Dedication

To
Eleri, Gildas, Trystan and Ffion

The Author

Gwyn Griffiths lives in the town of Pontypridd in South Wales. He became fascinated with Brittany in the mid-sixties and has returned there almost annually. He is the author of two volumes in Welsh on Brittany — a travel book entitled "Crwydro Llydaw" and "Y Shonis Olaf" which is a Welsh language version of this book. He has also translated plays from Breton into Welsh and contributed to many newspapers and periodicals, including some in Brittany and France.

A former journalist, he is employed by BBC Wales as its Senior Press and Public Relations Officer. He is 46, married with four children.

A Shoni-Onion Breton man, with a beret and a necklace of onions, bicycled down the road and stopped at the door.

''Quelle un grand matin, monsieur'' I said.

''There's French, boy bach!'' he said.

(from 'A Story' by Dylan Thomas)

Introduction

In my childhood no Autumn was complete without a call from Johnny Onions anymore than Spring was complete without the call of the cuckoo. I believed that we were somehow related even though he came from a distant land – after all he spoke my language (Welsh) very well. Alas, my Johnny and many others of that resilient breed have just about disappeared. I am told that their numbers dwindled to 15 in 1982.

I was fortunate to have found so many of them still prepared to talk to me so frankly about their experiences and memories. During September, October, November and December of 1977 I spent a great deal of time talking to Jean-Marie Cueff - sadly he died last year - and Olivier Bertevas. I did not know it at the time, but that was the last season for both of them on this side of the English Channel. Both talked freely about their lives, their worries and problems.

For the remainder of the material I visited Brittany and it was around Roscoff and St Pol de Leon that I spent September 1978 talking to as many retired onion sellers as I could find. They, too, gave me a warm welcome and every assistance.

After some thought I decided to relate the story as simply as possible, letting each retired Johnny tell his own story. I followed a similar pattern to present the material I gleaned from Cueff and Bertevas when they were in Cardiff. Between those two sections, I trust that here is a fairly honest view of the hardship and romance of the life and work of these men.

In the first section – where I try to set the background to this unique trade – I was fortunate to receive a copy from F. C. Kervella, Rennes, of an unpublished history of Roscoff.

While in Brittany I also had an opportunity to read parts of a thesis about the onion sellers offered by Jean-Jacques Moncus to the University of Brest (Moncus's father was one of Jean-Marie Cueff's colleagues in Brynmawr).

I received much useful assistance from my friend Bernard Le Nail, General Secretary of the Comité d'Etude et de Liaison des Intérêts Bretons, the Breton folk studies organization, Dastum, and one Johnny in particular, 'Peta-Claude' Corre.

May I hope that readers will experience a little of the pleasure and fun I enjoyed in the company of these remarkable characters.

Gwyn Griffiths.

1

The Annual Migration

It was, by all accounts, a fine day in 1828 when Henri Olivier, a sailor-peasant from the village of Santec set sail from the port of Roscoff in Brittany. His tiny boat was brimful of onions and with his four companions he sought the coast and markets of England. They had a fair wind behind them and in a couple of days they had arrived in Plymouth – a town their ancestors had plundered in 1405 – and were busily selling their produce. According to tradition they had no trouble selling their onions and in a very short time they were back in Roscoff, their belts crammed full of English money. But even more important, they had found a new market and given new hope to agriculture and commerce in that part of Roscoff and the surrounding countryside.

A new market? Well, not exactly. It is known that the Bretons had been trading with Britain since the Middle Ages and there had been considerable traffic between the countries in the Age of Saints. A written record exists of 26 Breton ships sailing to England between 1381 and 1391 and that four of these ships carried vegetables and farm produce. Nearly two centuries later in 1548, Mary Stuart landed in Roscoff engaged to be married to the boy who in 1559 was crowned Francois II of France and in October 1746, after the Battle of Culloden, the same port provided a haven for Bonnie Prince Charlie. The connection – frequently an uneasy one – between Britain and Roscoff continued with Roscoff being a centre for smugglers and pirates. In times of war, the ships of Roscoff were renowned for plundering English ships and on at least one occasion they led an attack on Bristol. One must assume, thus, that the English-Roscoff connection was frequently one where very little love was lost – one sign of this can be found in the tower of the church of Notre Dame Croaz Baz, Roscoff, with its two stone cannons a defiant warning to the occasional attacks of the 'perfide Albion'.

But despite old suspicions a thriving trade in cotton and linen existed over many centuries between England and this port on the north-western coast of Brittany. And when Henri Olivier landed in Plymouth in 1828 he was apparently received with enthusiasm.

Very little is known about Henri Olivier. Apparently he had been in search of new markets in Rennes and Paris before venturing to Plymouth – markets which might improve the economy of Roscoff and its countryside. Who knows that he did not possess similar ideas to Alexis Gourvennec, the founder of Brittany Ferries, who a century and a half later announced that he wanted to release the economy of Brittany from its heavy dependance on Paris and its beaurocracy and to bring about a closer relationship with the province's true historical partners, Britain and Ireland. However, for his historical journey to Plymouth Olivier co-operated with three neighbours to hire a boat and to ensure a supply of onions to sell. On the basis of that uneventful trip to Plymouth he deserves the title of 'The First Johnny Onions' – although this proved to be his only visit to England. It is said that he married a widow shortly afterwards – the suggestion is that she was comparatively wealthy – and that in due course they had three children. It might well be that he had no need to venture again, if the suggestion is really true that he married well.

The old trade in wool, linen and cotton had come to an end before Henri Olivier made his journey; competition from Northern France had killed off the industry in Brittany. By the 1820's there was little profit or purpose in illegal activities such as smuggling. So when the Roscovites learnt of the welcome which Olivier had received in Plymouth others were quick to follow in his footsteps. As seen from the testimony of many onion sellers recorded in a later chapter in this book, poverty was an important incitement for the annual migration in their youth.

It is not difficult to imagine how much greater that inducement and that poverty would have been in the Roscoff area in the twenties and thirties of the last century. Camille Vaullaux said of the low wages in the countryside around Roscoff and St Pol de Leon: 'There was an increase in wages in 1897 and now the *placenner* (the labourer who would loiter in the square hoping to be hired for a day's employment) in St Pol or

2

The tower of Notre Dame Croaz Baz, Roscoff. Note the two stone canons — a warning to the ''Perfide Albion''.

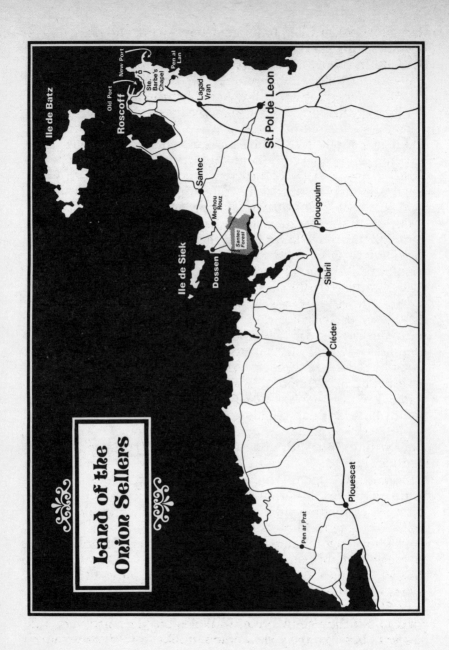

Land of the
Onion Sellers

Ile de Batz

Old Port · New Port
Roscoff · Ste. Barbe's Chapel
Pen al Lan

Lagad Vran

St. Pol de Leon

Santec

Mechou Rouz

Santec Forest

Ile de Siek

Dossen

Plougoulm

Sibiril

Cléder

Plouescat

Pen ar Prat

Roscoff could earn 1.19 francs for a day's work and there was no obvious change between 1897 and 1904. Yet in 1892 a worker on the land in North Finistere was paid 2.04 francs. The average wage for the whole territory was 2.57 francs'. *Mont diouz an deiz* (to go – for hire – by the day) had been the order of things for the men of this territory for many years.

Under such circumstances, it was not surprising that a new breed of people, later to be nick-named 'Johnnies' set about growing as much as the land could possibly yield and to sell that produce for the highest price possible. And there is no better soil anywhere for the cultivation of kitchen vegetables than this corner of Brittany. Having found markets the fertile fields of Roscoff and St Pol were well able to satisfy their demands. Henry Olivier found the market and the fertility of the land is evident for all to see. Linger casually in the countryside of Roscoff, St Pol de Leon, Plougoulm, Santec and Cleder and look at those acres heavy under crops of artichokes and cauliflowers. 'Here certainly', said Gustave Flaubert in 1847 'is the most fertile corner of Brittany. The Roscovite is a fortunate farmer, his field is his fortune'. And similarly, Emile Moraud in 1932 wrote that Roscoff is the most fertile of places and it has all the advantages for the growing of early vegetables. He added that the mild, humid, maritime climate is particularly suitable with the extensive continental shelf around the peninsula – with its shallow sea – providing a reservoir of warmth and a stable temperature. In general, the rain is fine and lasting, the 'Breton spit', which saturates the soil thoroughly.

Moraud says again 'The natural fertility, the climate and the value placed on the produce explains the success of "kitchen-garden" cultivation in the privileged zone of Roscoff and St Pol'. The magnificent harvests of onions, products of this exceptional soil, became the source by which the Johnnies tried to please the British housewives. Because the red onion of Roscoff is prized higher in London than in Paris. The French prefer the yellow onion grown around Langeux and Yffiniac, near St Brieuc. One Johnny told me that he and others once tried to sell the yellow onion in Wales but they had very little success – besides, the yellow onion, unlike the red, could not be

"The most fertile corner of Brittany", according to Gustave Flaubert. Acres of artichokes.

6

stored for long periods, an important factor for these importers.

The British are renowned for their love of the onion, but we produce only a small percentage of what we consume and those are frequently not of very high quality. Thus, the British import onions on a considerable scale – mostly from Egypt, from where the vegetable originates, Canada, Spain and Holland. The contribution of the Johnnies has never been great and by now the amount they bring to Britain is quite insignificant. Even in the golden era of the Johnnies one could almost say that the Breton contribution was of more interest because of the unique and colourful methods of the sellers than for the total quantity of onions sold.

But to return to Monsieur Olivier, there is no doubt that he was particularly fortunate in his choice of time to make his one and only visit to Plymouth. The population of Britain was on the increase as a result of the Industrial Revolution and British agriculture was unable to meet the demands of swiftly growing industrial towns. These were hard times for British agriculture with people leaving the land in droves to try and scrape a better living in the coal-mines and steel-works – the farming population of Britain dropped 29 per cent between 1881 and 1901 alone.

Britain was thus becoming more and more dependant on importing food. By the end of the last century Britain was importing food on as large a scale as any country in the world. Ten years after Henri Olivier made his historic journey the supporters of Free Trade were gathering momentum behind people like Richard Cobden and in 1842 the tax on goods imported into Britain was substantially reduced. Importing was further facilitated by crop failures in Britain – and more so in Ireland – in 1846. Then in 1849 Britain did away with the Trade Laws, which prevented ships from some foreign countries from bringing goods into British ports, and in 1853 the power of the customs was decreased.

With the turn of the century, a better understanding grew between Britain and France which provided a firm base for a substantial growth in the trade of the Onion Johnnies – a growth which came to a peak in the years between 1919 and

1930. This was the golden age of their trade. Although their numbers would fluctuate annually, depending mainly on the crops, it has been estimated that about 1,000 Johnnies came to Britain every year in the years leading up to World War I and that between 1,000 and 1,200 made the annual migration between 1920 and 1931. Indeed, I would not be surprised if these estimates are rather on the conservative side – particularly when one considers that as many as 14 Johnnies were coming to the small town of Newcastle Emlyn in the years leading up to World War II. Then, in the years prior to 1939 their numbers dropped to between 700 and 900 per year. The reasons for the decrease will be discussed later in this book.

Over the years the Johnnies migrated in a variety of ways and a variety of ships. Sailing ships were the most common form of transport for bringing the onions and the sellers over in the early days, and it is interesting and surprising to note that almost every onion seller that I interviewed had at one time or another crossed to Britain under sail – in ships with names like *L'Océanie, L'Hermann, Roscovite, La Bretonne* and *Jeune Olga* each carrying a load of anything between 30 and 120 tons each. One sailing ship continued to bring onions over as recently as 1952 although these ships were becoming fewer even as long ago as 1900. The steam ships, with their loads of between 300 and 500 tons came, and later the diesel ships.

The trade of the Johnnies ceased during World War I and similarly for the duration of World War II. But from the end of the first war until 1931 the trade and the annual migrations were at their greatest. The Johnnies would come in large groups or "companies", with each company having its own ship to export its onions. Frequently those ships would return to Brittany loaded with coal or some other commodity to come back to Britain almost immediately with another load of onions. This was the era of the schooners and the *great dundees* (a small ship which carried two masts, the rear being the smaller of the two) with names like *Kenavo, Araok, Sainte Anne* and *Jeanne*. In July and August of 1928 and 1929 it was a common sight to see as many as a dozen of these ships sailing out of Roscoff on the tide. This was of course in an age long before the new deep water port was established on the east side of the Roscoff

8

peninsula – the one used by Brittany Ferries.

Arrangements for the hire of boats for the onion sellers were prepared by people who acted as brokers or *transitaires* in Roscoff. The first of these was a Madame Guerc'h, the tenant of a restaurant in Roscoff who around 1830 started this traditon of hiring ships for the Johnnies to carry their onions – while keeping a very sharp eye on their interests at the same time. In time she also became their maritime agent, their banker, a judge to settle their disputes and broker. It was a natural development for the owners and tenants of restaurants and cafeés to do the administrative work for the onion sellers and to look after their interests. Was it not in the restaurants around the old port of Roscoff that the Johnnies discussed terms with their bosses, agreeing the details of their contracts over a meal and bottle of wine? Such a scene is described in a novel, *Johnny de Roscoff* by Yves-Marie Rudel, published by ''Librairie Celtique'' of Paris in 1945:

> ''The Café du Port was heaving. Another week and the first troop would be on their way to England; the onion sellers flocked around the tables and the air was thick with tobacco smoke. The merry company raised their glasses to Marie Johnniguet weaving her way amonst the tables exchanging a cheery word or two with her customers. She was the one who planned the journey for the Johnnies, following by letter the trials and tribulations of each one of her customers, some to the most remote corners of Britain. In this work she had taken the place of the old Anna, another fine organizer, if rough of speech; Anna who witnessed the departure of the first Johnnies, the departure of Henri Olivier and his friends a hundred years earlier''.

The tradition was perpetuated within families. Madame Guerc'h was succeeded by her daughter and, eventually, her grand-daughter. It was appropriate that when Madame Guerc'h's ancestral home was sold in 1936, it was bought by the port authority and used as a custom house. Other *transitaires* came to prominence in Roscoff, such as François Pichon and Charles Huart. It was common for the Johnnies to have representatives in British ports, too, who would ease arrangements with the customs authorities and arrange the transfer of money from British banks to banks in Brittany. There was a man called Shepherd who did this work in Swansea and another named Butt in Cardiff whom I heard mentioned by

A view of the old port of Roscoff from where the ships would sail to Britain in the old days.

Jean-Marie Cueff and Olivier Bertevas.

The day of departure was a great day. In an unpublished history of Roscoff I found the following description:

"It was one of the early days of July. The shreds of the mist, the herald of a warm day, lingered over the fields and the round heads of the artichokes. In the heart of the fertile Leon country, where the road from Cleder to St Pol paved in a mosaic of stone traces its long silvery ribbon, the wagons on their rubber tyres and heavily loaded with sacks full of onions glided with hardly a rustle behind the tinkling shoes of the horses.

A little further behind, like a rear guard or column, came the other carts carrying men, women and children in their Sunday clothes, seated astride the trunks, cases and packets of all kinds belonging to the men who would that day be embarking for England. The recently engaged "sevants" puffed up proudly in their new blue jerseys. They found the road long and the rhythm monotonous enough. And in order to pass the time they chatted about a wide variety of topics, happy conversations which they punctuated with heavy and hearty thumps on the thighs and shoulders of their neighbours.

By contrast the numbers of their families accompanying them replied in mono-syllables and seemed to wish to be unaware of their enthusiasm.

At St Pol they had a brief stop, just enough to stretch their legs to get a cup of coffee and a newspaper. Then they had the descent to Roscoff.

On arriving the women went their separate ways. Some went to the shops which had just opened for the day for some last minute shopping for their departing men, others went to the old church to light a candle in honour of Sainte Barbe and to offer a final prayer for those about to leave.

As to the servants who had made their agreements with their masters in advance at the house of Guivarch, Huard, Guerc'h or the sea broker Pichon, the day, at least until the next tide, was their own.

On the quays the waggons were emptied and the sacks of onions pushed down the slides into the boats but the waterfront cafes remained full. In Jean Huard's cafe, in "Ty Pierre" and all the cafes in Rue Gambetta, the red wine flowed, this was not a day to play dominoes, it was a day to drink, just drink.

Now that they were men amongst men, voices were raised. Fists thumped the tables causing glasses to overflow as the old campaigners recalled for the benefit of the young the salient points of the last campaign, the generous tips from some clients, the journey home to their quarters in the damp darkness and the thickening fog which causes you to stay close to the railings of the houses to avoid the tram-roads, the occasional bitter stout which would be followed the morning after by the hangover and the foul taste in the mouth, the

11

"miraculous", but most often imaginary sales, the tricks of the trade and the hundred other details about the life they would soon experience. The young servants having received that verbal initiation, went each his own way. They picked up their boxes, already with the feverish look of those about to enter a trade full of the unforeseen.

Their parents, then their friends, came to join them and to raise a glass with them a final time, but not to participate much in the general enthusiasm which increased as the bottles emptied.

Then came the hour to depart. In a rattle of sabots, a chorus of chants and laughs, the troop poured in disorder into the port's narrow streets and rolled towards the "Amphitrite", a composite schooner with an ornate bow in a form of a wife of Neptune artistically evoking the old days of wooden ships.

The embarking dragged on: embraces, final advice by mothers to the young. Then, in heavy silence, the final sail is freed. The Johnnies file aboard, shouldering their boxes, while on the pier wives and children waved their handkerchiefs. They then began moving towards the Chapel of Sainte Barbe, arriving at the sanctuary at the same time as those departing, who following their tradition struck up the old verses of 'Santez Barba' in their broad Breton. Then they struck up the anthem of the men of Roscoff: "N'eus par e Breiz Izel da baotred Rosco..."

On the grey stones of the quay, the tiny figures gradually disappear... soon the two groups will have disappeared entirely from each other's view as the distance separating them increases.

In a very short time, the Johnnies are well on their way: a fair wind pushing them towards England. They will be back in their homes in time for Christmas."

While the women raised their voices in praise of Sainte Barbe around the little chapel on the hill their husbands in the boats did the same. As they slid between the tiny isle of Ty-Saozan (the house of the English) and the hillock on which stands the chapel of Sainte Barbe the sailing ships would slow down and the engines of the steamers would be silenced. Each ship would lower its banner in a gesture of respect to the patron saint of the onion sellers in the time honoured way. Within three days they would be in Portsmouth or Southampton or one of the other ports on the south coast of England. Others faced a longer journey, for those making their way to Aberdeen it was not unusual for them to be at sea for a fortnight or more. In the words of the song 'Paotred Rosko' (The Lads of Roscoff): "Mont a rein hebdale betek penn ar bed" (They will go without hesitation to the far corners of the world).

Sainte Barbe's chapel, where the wives prayed as their husbands sailed away.

13

Camille Vallaux in 1907 also held the lads of Roscoff in high esteem: "Le Roscovite est le commerçant par excellence". As has already been noted, the seasonal migrations of the Johnnies were due to economic and historical reasons. It was an area which suffered real poverty and the town of Roscoff had its tradition of trading – a tradition inherited by the Johnnies. When Henri Olivier discovered a new market and gave rise to new methods of selling in Britain the Johnnies set about producing as much as the soil could grow and then went to sell the produce for the highest possible price. The onion seller proved that he had a spirit for adventure and the cheek to be a success. He also knew how to turn on the charm necessary to sell his onions from door to door and he proved that his temperament was a curious composition of toughness and cunning.

He was also a persistent salesman – if he found the door slammed in his face he would come knocking at the window. There was no way in which he could be disarmed, nothing would repel him. Such effrontery often flabbergasted the English. This persistence developed at a time when every Johnny had to compete with many other Johnnies all from the same tiny area of North Western Brittany. It was a persistence that was to earn him the nick-name of "bell-breaker". If he did not get an answer he would pull at the door-bell until it broke! But this century he became a far more popular visitor who every year received a cordial welcome in whatever part of the United Kingdom he appeared. His new nick-name became a term of endearment and he himself a figure of immense popularity who was received sympathetically. This was no noisy market or fair-ground hawker, but a reticent man who had learnt that his customers were prepared to run after him – particularly in recent years. He gained the reputation of being a kind of cheerful beggar who did not beg, but who worked hard to earn his daily crust.

Up to the year 1930 the Johnnies operated in fairly large groups or "companies". Sometimes as many as 30 belonged to one company. Then, they had to face a number of set-backs. The pound was devalued in 1931-32 and in February 1932 an import duty of ten per cent was placed on foreign goods brought into the United Kingdom but giving special concessions to Commonwealth countries, under the Ottawa agreement, which came into force in 1932. These factors had a considerable effect on the trade of the Johnnies and the "companies" were split into small groups. Instead of a single "company" hiring an entire ship to bring over their onions and their sellers, one ship would now be seen bringing over as many as 30 "companies" on a single journey. The onion loads that were brought across the channel became smaller and the Johnnies decreased in numbers. Between 1932 and 1939 the numbers of Johnnies were reduced to between 700 and 900 a season. And naturally, the tonnage of onions exported to Britain was reduced.

In 1860 it has been estimated that a 1,000 tons of onions were landed on these shores; by 1908 the figures had risen to 7,906; by the First World War it was nearly 10,000 tons. The trade restarted modestly after the war and in 1921 2,572 tons were brought to Britain. The total increased steadily and by 1927 it had reached 9,710 tons and it remained thereabouts until 1931. Then, with the devalued pound, the new import duties and the effects of the 'Buy British' movement, the Johnny Onions trade suffered a huge slump. In 1932 a mere 3,245 tons were brought over by them, it dropped to 2,786 in 1933 before rising again to about 4,500 in 1936. Prices were higher in 1937 and there were signs of better times ahead, but due to the low prices of the previous year the onion growers lost enthusiasm and had not produced sufficient quantities and in a very short time all the 2,203 tons of onions exported to Britain had been sold.

After World War II the Johnnies found themselves facing a long, hard fight to re-establish their trade on the same basis as they had enjoyed before the war. Following the war years, the British government in 1947 tried to encourage the continuation of high food production in order to keep imports as low as possible. Also, the pound was devalued again in 1949. Faced with these problems the Johnnies began a long battle to regain their traditional market. This was not going to be an easy battle, because the Ministry of Food, in order to aid British argiculture, had imposed special regulations to restrict the importing of fresh fruit and vegetable. Foreign importers were prohibited to

15

retail their products in any part of the United Kingdom. This simply prohibited the Johnnies from emigrating – it was a prohibition that threatened the destruction of their method of trading.

But if the Breton is renowned for anything it's his pig-headedness and he needed every ounce of his fierce Roscovite obstinacy to regain the right to import as many tons of onions into Britain as he wished and on the terms he had enjoyed before 1939 – namely complete freedom apart from his import duty.

It was not until 1954, after a long and bitter battle during which time they had no certainty from year to year what quantities and on what terms they would be allowed to sell during the coming season, that their problem was resolved. A key figure in this nine year conflict was François Mazeas, born in 1911 and who retired from selling onions in 1952. Mazeas's request to re-start his trade at the end of 1945 was refused by the British Government. But he was not a man to give up easily. He went to Paris and for a fortnight he knocked on the doors of the *Ministère de l'Agriculture,* the *Ministère des Finances et des Affaires Economiques* and the *Centre National du Commerce Extèrieur* (C.N.C.E.). He was sent from office to office, from floor to floor, from department to department; nobody in Paris had ever heard of the men of Roscoff who went every year to sell their onions in Britain. Finally, at the C.N.C.E., he caught the ear of the department responsible for providing agricultural advice. Mazeas must have been very persuasive because an appointment was made for him with the trade counsellor close to the French Ambassador in London. Mazeas went to 22 Hans Place, London, where he met the commercial attaché, M. Mareschal, who promised to help and to plead personally the cause of the Johnnies in the offices of the relevant British Ministries. He kept his word and proved to be one of the Johnnies' most faithful and efficient supporters.

Fortunately for the Bretons , the British onion growers in 1946 had a particularly disastrous harvest and this caused the goverment at very short notice to authorise the importation of a large tonnage of onions from the Roscoff area. The Johnnies were caught unawares by this sudden change of heart by the

16

British Government, but they moved quickly and profited handsomely from this unexpected windfall. A number of substantial loads were dispatched from Roscoff in the middle of February 1947, but the Johnnies were not allowed to sell the onions in their traditional way on this occasion – this had to be done by British retailers.

It was the only occasion when the onion sellers brought their onions to the United Kingdom but did not retail them in their time honoured method.

To record the full details of what happened in the ensuing years would take many chapters, instead it will suffice for me to note some of the most important events in this episode. A significant and necessary step was the establishment of the *Association des vendeurs d'oignons de Roscoff et de sa région*, in October 1947. The association was established at the request of the Ministry of Food in London which insisted that if it was to negotiate with the onion sellers it had to be through an organization which represented them. It was not unexpected that the first president of the Association was François Mazeas. After the Association had been established on lines acceptable to the British authorities, the Johnnies were allowed to take up their traditional trade again for the following season, but there were certain conditions:

1. The total amount to be imported to Britain for the 1947-48 season would be limtied to 2,500 tons.

2. Licences would be attributed only to those Johnnies who had practised the trade before the War. In fact, membership of the *Association des vendeurs l'oignons de Roscoff et de sa région* was limited to those who had been onion sellers before the War. The licence was valid for three months.

3. The price of sale in Britain was fixed by an order, dated November 6, 1947, to a maximum of $4\frac{1}{2}$d a pound. To this purpose every seller had to be in possession at all times of a spring scale (*eur stillen* as the Johnnies called it) which he would have to produce if asked by an Inspector of Weights and Measures.

4. The onions sold in Britain had to be harvested in France by the seller or his employer. It was prohibited for any seller to buy the onions, or other similar products (i.e. garlic or shallots) with a view to resell them in Britain.

Any merchant caught selling his merchandise above the price of 4½d a pound or who contravened any of the conditions stipulated by the Ministry would be liable to prosecution in a British court.

There was also a limitation placed on when onions could be brought into Britain by the Johnnies. But despite all these restrictions the Johnnies were in a far better position than onion growers in other parts of France. In December 1948 the onion growing industry throughout France was in a desperate plight; there was no way in which the growers could sell their produce. The only district able to sell its onions was that of Roscoff, thanks to the very special understanding which existed between the Johnnies and the British government and to a tradition that spanned 120 years. But the restrictions on the Roscoff onion sellers were still considerable and Mazeas, aided by Mareschal, fought on to try and get for the Johnnies the freedom they had enjoyed before the war. Gradually the restrictions were eased. In 1950 only one remained – namely that no onions could be imported to Britain from Roscoff between August 15 and November 15. Then in 1954 after many lengthy letters and arguments, with the tireless Mazeas and Mareschal at the forefront of the fight, the old trade was restored to its traditional freedom. The only restriction being the toll paid when the onions were brought through the British ports. The obstinate Breton had won the battle but it had been a victory gained too late in the day. The following year, Mazeas suffered a serious leg injury which meant that he could no longer go on the annual migration to Britain. But he remained President of the "Association of the onion sellers of Roscoff and district" until 1958. But it is sad to have to note that those nine years of uncertainty after World War II probably drove some telling nails into the coffin of this unique and colourful trade.

The British Government had no objection to the Johnnies and the total amount of onions imported by them through our ports certainly never threatened the farmers of this country in any way. It was a case of the Johnnies suffering from laws aimed at safeguarding British agriculture, laws which quite naturally paid scant attention to the trade of the Johnnies – a trade often more colourful than efficient, more original than economic.

18

By now, Johnny Onions has almost vanished for ever from our streets and countryside. The Autumn and Winter of 1977-78 saw Jean-Marie Cueff and Olivier Bertevas tramping the streets of Cardiff and the valleys of south-east Wales for the last time – for five or six years they had been insisting to every one of the many journalists who interviewed them that they were making positively their last trip to this country. But no one ever really believed them and it was with some surprise and a lot of sadness that their regular customers realised in September 1978 that they had finally kept their word. And so, throughout Britain the old hawkers tire and call it a day. Although two youngsters from Plouescat and Brest have since started coming to Cardiff the youngsters, generally speaking, do not replace the old. Their numbers decrease from year to year. Even before these words see the light of day we may well have seen the end of a tradition started over a century and a half ago. Even the unique red onion of Roscoff itself is in danger of disappearing – as the requirements of the Johnnies decrease less and less land is devoted annually to its cultivation. Once the day of the Johnnies is over there will no longer be a market for the red onion – the French as has already been stated prefer the yellow onion. And as the vicious circle of decline continues one wonders whether it will be a scarcity of onions or a scarcity of sellers which will be the final cause for the disappearance of the last of the Breton onion sellers.

With the passing of time, the children have turned their backs on the trade of the fathers, indeed it is the grandfathers who now almost entirely maintain what remains of this tradition – men approaching their seventieth birthday. Quite naturally, the young were not satisfied with the lack of security of the trade of their fathers, particularly the uncertainty of these years immediately following World War II. Also in the past, before Britain joined the Common Market, there was no satisfactory insurance to safeguard the Johnnies should they suffer an accident or illness. Another disadvantage I discovered from my talks with the old onion sellers was that while they were abroad they could not contribute towards their pension. In some cases the onion sellers who owned their own small-holdings and were self-employed managed to overcome this problem. ''The

19

authorities just had no idea where I was. As far as they knew I was at home going about my business on the farm and I made sure that I paid my contributions." But there is no doubt that many of the old Johnnies are now receiving a smaller pension than they deserve because of this rule and no doubt the youngsters were aware of this drawback. It also became easier for those in need of employment to migrate to other parts of France for the winter months – more money could be made in the sugar factories and problems such as contributing to a pension fund did not then arise. In many ways they were also nearer home.

With the war years being followed by a further nine years of uncertainty there was a total of fifteen years which restricted opportunities for new onion sellers to become involved in the trade. Between 1939 and 1954 very few new recruits joined the annual migration. A basic necessity for the trade of the Johnnies was a knowledge of English (with the exception of those who sold their onions in Welsh speaking Wales and who learnt Welsh instead). Middle aged people cannot cope so easily with learning a new language – the young learn a new language far more easily. When Jean-Marie Cueff came over for the first time he was only nine years of age. Today, people would certainly not look favourably on an onion seller who brought his entire family – babies and all – to live in an old store house or dilapitated shop in the cold and damp of an English winter.

It has also been said that a special relationship grew between buyer and seller. Over the years they became great friends and when a housewife found that her Johnny was no longer coming over she was not quite so ready to buy from another – she would prefer to go to her local supermarket to buy her onions, usually at a cheaper price, too. Many a new Johnny realized that there was more to "chiner" * than he had dreamt – a technique had to be learnt. Despite Britain's entry into the Common Market and the establishment of Brittany Ferries with its new deep water port at Roscoff the new developments came too late to save the Johnnies.

In the main it has been left to the old men to close the last chapter in the history of the Roscoff onion trade. We shall no doubt see another trade, more suitable to the age of the EEC,

* Selling from door to door.

flourishing between Britain and Brittany. But it will hardly be more colourful or interesting.

Jean-Marie Cueff. He came to Cardiff for the last time in 1977.

2
Disasters

The restrictions following World War II were a serious blow, a disaster, to the trade of the Johnnies. But there were two disasters of a different kind, far more terrible, in the 150 year history of the onion-sellers, two occasions when a frighteningly large number of them, particularly when one considers the tiny area from which they came, lost their lives in shipwrecks.

The first of these occurred on February 1, 1898 when the *Channel Queen* sank on its route from Plymouth to Brittany. About 18 onion-sellers were lost in that disaster. The second disaster, when the *Hilda* sank in 1905 was much worse when a total of 74 Johnnies lost their lives.

There were 44 onion-sellers, 26 from Falmouth and 18 from Exeter, returning to Brittany on the *Channel Queen* when the ship struck a rock near Guernsey and sank. There is some uncertainty regarding the number of Bretons who were drowned but the most likely figure appears to be 18. The disaster happened on Tuesday morning, February 1, 1898 about 5.00 a.m. The *Channel Queen* which belonged to *The Plymouth, Channel Islands and Brittany Steamship Company* had left Plymouth about 11.00 p.m. the previous night. She was a 385 ton steamer, 177 feet long, 24 feet wide and 10 feet deep and has been described as being the largest and best appointed passenger ship on the service between Plymouth and the Channel Islands. She had been built in Middlesborough in 1895 and was a doublescrew ship. After the *Channel Queen* set sail from Plymouth on Monday, January 31 a dense fog descended which became even worse as the night progressed. The onion-seller who had been saved told a correspondent of the *Matin* of Guernsey:

> "There were two groups of us onion-sellers, the first consisted of 18 persons, the second of 36. We were returning to Brittany after a stay in England of anything between one and six months... the *Channel Queen* contained a crew of 19 and a total of 48 passengers, three of whom travelled first class.
>
> "The ship had made its journey unhindered. Some of us were sleeping in the stores, others were out on the bridge, when suddenly, the engines stopped. It was about 5.00 a.m.

22

"We hit a rock. The water penetrated the hold, and it was evident that the vessel was sinking rapidly. The two lifeboats were put to sea. The first capsized and the seven passengers, who had got into it, hung desperately to the keel but could not be saved by the other boat. The second lifeboat with nine of our compatriots arrived on the shore.

"The local fishermen, informed of the disaster, came directly to our aid, but the rocks were so dangerous that the rescuers had to keep their distance. They threw ropes and lifebelts to us. During this time the water sweeping the port side washed away some of our compatriots who disappeared for ever. One wave plucked a child from the arms of its mother".

It was some time before the full details were known. According to the captain, whose name was Collings, the number of passengers on the *Channel Queen* was 40. But as is seen in the case of the sinking of the *Hilda*, captains and shipping authorities were never sure exactly how many passengers were on board. They were only certain of the number of first-class passengers. Speaking to the *Matin* Collings said: "Towards 5.00 a.m. the *Channel Queen* hit a rock, rebounded heavily and rested immoveably on the 'Black Rock', a mile from the coast and half a mile from the great Havre". He did not leave the ship until the water was almost up to his armpits.

A few days later the people who had lost their lives began to be named. On February 3 information indicated that 18 of the victims had French or Breton names in addition to six members of the crew who were also lost. The list of drowned onion-sellers included a boy aged 10, a 13 year old, one 14 year old, a 16 year old and a 19 year old.

On February 16 the steamer *L'Aber* took those who had been saved following the *Channel Queen* disaster to St Brieuc. As could be expected there was grave concern in Roscoff and St Pol as families waited for news of their relatives. Lives had been lost as were substantial sums of money on which many Breton families depended until next year's migration. To make matters worse, neither the passengers nor the money they had on their persons was insured.

Alas, they did not profit from their grim experience and seven years later, in 1905, many more onion-sellers were drowned in what was a far worse tragedy. A little before midnight on

The "Hilda" steaming out of St. Malo. It was on the return journey that the disaster occurred.

Saturday, November 18, 1905, the *Hilda* sank on her way into St Malo with the loss of 125 lives, 74 of whom were Breton onion-sellers. The Johnnies were on their way home after a season selling their onions and the money they had on them went to the bottom of the channel.

The 848 ton steamship *Hilda* belonged to the *London and South Western Railway Company*. On Friday, November 17, 1905, at about 10.00 p.m., the *Hilda* left Southampton for St Malo. According to the figures of *Lloyd's Register of Shipping* she carried a total of 131 persons, 79 of whom were Breton onion-sellers. There were 24 other passengers and a crew of 28 under the command of captain William Gregory. She was due to have left Southampton at 8.15 p.m. but was delayed at the outset by dense fog and lay off Yarmouth, Isle of Wight, until the following morning. *Lloyd's Register Of Shipping* says "The *Hilda* left the Isle of Wight at about 6.00 a.m., the weather being fine and clear until early afternoon when she encountered a series of snow squalls, with rising wind and sea. By about 6.00 p.m. the vessel had reached the Chenal de Petite Porte at the entrance to St Malo, but here she met another blinding snow squall and put about for open sea until the weather cleared. For the next five or six hours she lay off the coast waiting for an opportunity to make harbour. At some time during this period she must have been headed shorewards, for just before midnight she struck on a reef known as the Pierres des Portes".

According to *The Times* of Monday, November 20, 1905 the *Hilda* ought to have reached St Malo about 6.00 a.m. on the morning of Saturday. "Though as the morning advanced there was no appearance of the vessel, no particular anxiety was felt, because it was known that a snowstorm was raging in the Channel on the French side, and the *Hilda* had the reputation of being a first-class seagoing boat... As the day wore on, the absence of any tidings of the vessel gave rise to a concern which increased every hour".

When the *Hilda* struck the Pierres des Portes the first boat was lowered but it was smashed before it reached the water and before the others could be got away the ship broke in two, the stern portion going down with most of the passengers.

Reuter's reported from St Servan in Brittany:

"The majority of the crew and passengers were asleep in their bunks when the *Hilda* struck, and so there was no time for everybody to come on deck and help to lower the boats. Two boats were, however, lowered and one of them with five men has arrived here. The second has been picked up empty at St Cast, where 13 bodies have been washed ashore. It is supposed that they belonged to the *Hilda*. Four more bodies have been picked up at the scene of the disaster by steamers sent from St Malo and brought here this afternoon. Four of the men saved are onion-sellers and the fifth belonged to the crew. The names of the missing are not known. The top of the *Hilda's* funnel and one mast are visible at low water".

The sole survivor from the crew of 28, Able Seaman James Grinter recalled his experiences to a *Daily Mail* reporter, an account which appeared in the paper's November 22 issue:

"... There was a terrible snowstorm and suddenly a horrible shock went right through the ship followed by the sound of friction. I think that it was about midnight.
"Within minutes I was on the bridge. In spite of the darkness I could see the spiky rocks. The captain ordered the boats be put to sea. The ship rolled terribly and with every movement ran onto rocks... The French onion-sellers helped to put the life-belts on the women. As the ship leaked I was struck by the apparent calm of everyone. We were in a vortex of snow as the ship sank. I was flung into the rigging and I climbed the great mast with the mate. There were about 20 people in the rigging when the boat sank.
"The mate held on until 6.00 a.m. and then fell headlong into the water... At day-break we could see the rocks and I saw the *Ada*".

The *Ada* was a steamship belonging to the same company as the *Hilda*. The *Ada* should have sailed from St. Malo on Friday night but because of the storm and the danger of colliding with the *Hilda* in the channel the captain postponed sailing until day-break on Sunday, November 19. The *Ada* set sail at 8.00 a.m. and in a short time the captain, through his telescope, witnessed the terrible results of the disaster. He saw the ship's masts on the Pierres des Portes which are some four miles from St Malo and slightly less than half a mile from the lighthouse called the "Grand Jardin". He realised instantly that it was the *Hilda* and he ordered that the life-boats be put to sea immediately.

One of the Johnnies who survived, Olivier Caroff of Roscoff, reported the events in rather greater detail than Grinter and his story conflicted with that of the sailor particularly as regarded the apparent calm. He was reported in the St Malo *Chronique* (November 24, 1905) as saying:

"... The memory of that terrible night is a nightmare. I had been asleep before the disaster but I woke suddenly from the cold. I got up. It was pitch dark, I couldn't see beyond four metres. I walked towards the bridge where I saw the captain giving orders. 'Filthy weather' I said to a passing sailor; we must have been close to St Malo, but I couldn't see the lighthouse.

"A little later, I think that I glimpsed a glimmer of light. The "Great Jardin" lighthouse is green, white, and red. The boat siren whistled violently, the alarm bell sounded. I thought of returning to my bed when there was a tremendous shock through the boat which hurled me backwards. I got up and ran towards the stern. I ran into the mast. The ship was sinking. I started climbing the mast.

"Then I saw people running wildly. Men were climbing all around me. I hastened to get up there, the higher the better. There was terrible cracking, a rumbling sound, the centre of the ship disappeared and sank. I heard shrieks which made by blood run cold.

"There were a score of us on the mast. Every so often one of us fell off. The cold was getting to me. How much time did I pass thus? I cannot say. When day came, I saw the smoke, a black mass: it was the *Ada*: life! The boatswain's mate Morel arrived with sailors in a boat. I don't remember any more until I woke up in hospital in their warm sheets. That morning I gave thanks that I was alive".

It is interesting also to read the account pieced together by Dr. Tuloup in his *Saint Malo – Histoire General* published in 1965:

"The snow storm was violent, one could not see beyond five metres... Captain Gregory who had been in command of the ship for many years, certainly knew the danger and wished to stay well off Cazembre, but the passengers who had suffered from the heavy weather were so insistent that they be taken into St Malo that, against his better judgement, he decided to cross these at the best of times very dangerous channels. In such weather this was an extremely treacherous crossing. It was midnight. The winking white, green and red light of the Tour du Jardin could no longer be seen, neither the winking white of the Noires of St Malo nor the Balue which indicated the route to follow. He took the wrong route.

"His ship ripped itself on the rocks and the furious waves shattered it in two. The front part rested on the Roc des Plates which constituted the main danger in that channel. The other part sank. The passengers had all put on their life-jackets. They floated thus as the fury of the waves carried them towards the shore. The freezing cold had not spared them. The following morning, at St Cast, 69 corpses, kept upright by their life-jackets, were carried to the shore on the current. It was a sight which struck terror into the hearts of the local people".

The *Daily Mail* correspondent in St Malo wrote on Tuesday, November 21:

"Returning by the wreck this evening at low tide, I was able to visit it, for the front part, completely broken off, is perched prow upwards on a jagged rock. It was evidently steaming full speed at the time of the accident. Ten yards to the left of the rock and the *Hilda* would have steamed safely through an open channel".

A *Daily Mail* special correspondent in St Cast on the same day described the scenes in that small town:

"The scene at St Cast beggars description, so heartrending is it. All the bodies have now been placed in the old church, whose door is draped in black with the French and English flags flying at half-mast. The church bell is tolling continually, and Mass succeeds Mass. The old church is full of flowers and wreaths, and is crowded with relations and friends of the victims.

"The grief of the Breton women is terrible to witness. One of them beats her breast, continually calling out, 'Ma doue! Ma doue!' and bending down to kiss the face of her only son. One woman, on entering the church, recognising three brothers and her husband, fainted away.

"One can hear nothing but wailing and cries of distress. One man, half mad with grief, is calling to his brother – a corpse – and wringing him by the hand.

"Many are washing the faces of their dead with holy water. The cure is consoling the relations, but they are all half mad with grief. In front of the church are roughly-constructed coffins scattered about waiting for the identifications to be completed.

"No more bodies have yet been discovered. The wind has changed and local sailors think they are being carried out to sea, and may not be found for days. I have inspected the belongings of the victims, and nearly every watch stopped at a quarter to twelve. Only one watch had stopped at 11.30".

The *Daily Mail* correspondent in St Malo described a visit he had just made to St Cast as "one of the saddest scenes in life". He continued:

"Be it said to the credit of the inhabitants of this out-of-way place that, although most of the corpses had sums varying from £25 to £200 in English gold in belts round their waists, and although even in some cases the gold was found scattered, it was gathered and laid on the body to which it was nearest. The worthy Bretons scorned to rob the dead".

When the *Ada* boats arrived at the scene of the disaster, only five survivors were found, all clinging, cramped with cold to the *Hilda's* rigging. Four of them were Johnnies, Olivier Caroff of Roscoff, Paul Marie Pern of Cleder, Tanguy Laot of Cleder, Louis Rozec of Plouzevede and the sailor James Grinter. Louis Mouster of La Feuillée was picked up later on a neighbouring islet where he had been walking non-stop in an effort to get some warmth into his body. He had seen his brother-in-law being plucked away to his death by the waves.

The other survivors had similar stories to relate. Pern had climbed the rigging with a 14 year old boy, Calarnou of Cleder, on his back. The teenager died of exposure. Another Cleder man, whose surname was Velly, also died from the cold.

How many Johnnies were there on the *Hilda*? According to the Lloyd's Register of Shipping there was a total of 131 people on the ship, 79 of them onion-sellers, 24 other passengers and a crew of 28. At the time it proved a difficult task to discover exactly how many people had been on the ship. *The Times* correspondent in Southhampton on November 19 telegraphed that "the crew numbered 26; and there were 20 ordinary passengers and 54 onion men". As the majority of the Johnnies were travelling third-class there was no list of their names. Reuter's Agency reported from St Servan on the same day that 123 lives had been lost. At St Malo it was being estimated that there were 60 onion-sellers on the ship. But it was not until the bodies were floating ashore in frightening numbers that an accurate assessment could be made of the magnitude of the tragedy. It was announced on November 21 that the sea had yielded 60 bodies on the beach of St Cast, 15 in Plevenou, 2 in St Jacut and 5 in St Malo. Among the bodies discovered on the beach of St Cast was that of Captain William Gregory. On November 22 came further news from St Cast that on board the *Hilda* there had been "besides the first and second class passengers and crew, 82 onion merchants, all of Finistère. 77 are dead of whom 44 are from the single commune of Cleder".

At Roscoff, no one knew exactly the number of onion-selling companies who had embarked on the *Hilda*. Many of the Johnnies had written in their letters that they would be sailing

Saint-Malo — Naufrage du " HILDA " (Nuit du 18 au 19 novembre 1905)
Scaphandriers recherchant les cadavres

The ship-wrecked "Hilda" and local people looking for survivors on the following day.

either on Saturday or Sunday. Evidently there was great consternation at Roscoff, which was made all the greater by the general uncertainty and confusion. The *St Malo Chronique* reported that there were many onion-sellers in England at the time. Representatives from Roscoff were sent to St Malo to get information as to who had been drowned.

A rumour spread that the Johnnies were carrying large sums in gold about their persons and as a result the authorities gave orders for strict surveillance of the coasts to prevent any plundering. One rumour claimed that some of the Johnnies had as much as 50,000 francs on them – but it was discovered that the figure was between 2,800 and 15,000 francs.

The identification of the corpses caused many heart-rending scenes. A Madame Kerbiriou from Roscoff found the bodies of her two sons, Eugene, aged 13 and Jean, 17. A Madame Calarnou died on November 25 when she found the remains of her 14 year old son. The bodies of two Pichon brothers were identified by their sister who later found her husband, too, among the dead. On the Monday following the disaster two young men from Roscoff walked in their crude clogs all the way to St Cast to see if they would find their father's body among the corpses. They did not find his remains there and they continued to St Malo where they arived at 6.00 p.m. on the Wednesday, having walked 184 kilometres in 48 hours. The poor wretches, not having the money to take a train had not hesitated to undertake that journey to try and give their father a proper burial.

By the evening of November 22 all the bodies had been recognized with the exception of two, an English woman and an onion-seller whose first name, Guillaume, only was known. More information emerged. All 20 members of the company of J. M. Calarnou, Cleder, 12 of them from Cleder, 6 of Plouescat and 2 of Plougoulm were lost. Similarly, the company of 25 year old Paul Jaouen which numbered 13 – 5 from Plouescat, 5 from Cleder and 3 others whose place of birth is no longer known – were all drowned. In the company of Louis Quiviger from Cleder, 14 were drowned and two saved. Again the majority of the company came from Cleder. Louis Tanguy of Sibiril was drowned as were his sons Guillaume, aged 25, Claude, 18 and

François, 14. The company of the Pichon brothers from Roscoff consisted of 17 members – 7 from Roscoff, 3 from Sibiril, 3 from La Feuillée, 2 from St Pol, one from Plouenan and one from Plougoulm. Fourteen were drowned, one was saved and it was later discovered that two had not embarked at Southampton. One of them had suddenly felt a desire to have a look at the town before sailing and then missed the boat – for three days his parents had believed him to be dead. The other had gone celebrating, which he did with too much enthusiasm, and was picked up by the police in a drunk and disorderly conditions. He remained grateful to the Southampton police for the rest of his life.

There was no insurance in those days and as well as the lives lost the earnings on which many a family depended for a whole year had gone to the bottom of the sea. The district faced terrible poverty. But a number of funds were launched to help the families of the drowned – one was set up by students in Rennes and another by a newspaper, *Le Gaulois*. The Mayor of Southampton started a fund and another was established by the Chambre of French Commerce in London.

Cleder was the place which suffered most. Of those who were lost, 44, over half the entire drowned came from that village. It is hardly surprising that the number of Johnnies who ventured across the channel in the next few years dropped considerably. But gradually the trade picked up to reach its golden age after World War I and the parents and children of some of the victims of the *Hilda* disaster were seen going towards Bro Zaoz (as the Bretons call England) ''da werza da'r Zaozon gwella vouen ougnon zo''. (To sell to the English onions which have no better).

3

Two Onion-Men in Cardiff

"No home, no comforts, walking through wind and rain in all weather. Getting soaked, and having to remain in those clothes from morning to night. Eating cold onions, and the occasional crust of dry bread. And Sunday, it's the saddest day of all for us when we're in Wales. No Cathedral like the one in St Pol. No praying or singing Breton and Latin... And no dressing up for Sunday... Many people in Wales think that we're tramps".
(An onion-seller speaking to Welsh writer Ambrose Bebb in the 30's).

Bute Street in Cardiff has a certain notoriety and not a little romance. To the valley boys it conjured visions of a 'red light' district, a place where policemen always walked in twos if not in threes. Number 253 was a condemned shop in the end of Bute Street nearest the centre of Cardiff, the windows had been smashed and boarded-up. It was one of the last sections of the famous street to be demolished and replaced by new flats and houses. A little lower down is the new Salvation Army hostel and I recall the remains of the old hostel nearby with faded signs advertizing "Good Food" and "Clean Beds" as well as demolition warnings. Any shops used and occupied at the end of the 70's had strong bars across their windows.

For the five months from September to January 1977-78, 253 Bute Street provided shelter and a storehouse for Jean-Marie Cueff and Olivier Bertevas on what was to prove their last visit selling onions in Cardiff. This was their base, whether they wheeled their onion laden bicycles through the streets of Cardiff or whether they hired a car to pay a swift visit to Brynmawr, Merthyr, Bridgend, Aberdare or Ystrad Mynach. Their pronunciation of the Welsh place names is perfect and their accent pure valleys but with a slight French "soupçon". Alone, they always speak Breton, the gruff accents of true "Leonards".

In what would have been the shop area of the building, sacks of onions are stacked tidily almost to the ceiling. In a corner a potage of meat, onions and potatoes simmers gently on a camping stove. Nearby is an empty bottle with *rouge ordinaire* on

Jean-Marie Cueff and Olivier Bertevas in Cardiff.

the label; it has probably been empty for days if not weeks but it remains unrinsed. In the back room the two are stringing onions. They use rushes and bits of raffia. A few days earlier they had been to the outskirts of Cardiff cutting rushes. "We have to cut it ourselves and pay for it, and we have to hire a lorry to fetch it" says Jean-Marie. He appears rather unfriendly. "We have to pay our way at all times". "It cost us £300 to hire a lorry to bring our onions over" says Olivier. He is a smaller man, milder and appears far more pleasant than his aggressive comrade as he strings his onions in his slippers. Cueff interrupted quickly "What the hell do you want to tell him how much we paid? I don't ask him what he paid for his car. I know he has two children, but it's no business of mine. I mind my own business and I don't want people pushing their noses into mine". It's a little difficult to decide whether his apparent surliness is genuine or not. We converse in a mixture of English, Breton and French. Breton is certainly their usual language of conversation. After Breton they appear to be more at home in English than French. Certainly we use French less frequently than the other two languages. They string the onions rapidly without interrupting their conversation – six or seven rushes, a piece of raffia, a large onion at the bottom as an anchor, then small onions round the bottom of the string with larger onions as they get near the top. Two single strings are then tied together to make a double string which can be draped over the handlebars of a bicycle. There is no sign of a scale but I feel certain that if we were to weigh a number of strings they would be almost identical in weight. The neat row of strung onions grows quickly. Jean-Marie – he is called Jimmy by his customers in Cardiff – said that they never spoke anything to each other except Breton. "I speak only Breton to my children" he added "But they mostly answer me in French". It's a familiar story in Brittany. Both know a few phrases of Welsh even though neither has ever worked in Welsh-speaking Wales.

Olivier certainly knows a lot about Welsh language developments and named a number of Welsh medium primary schools in the valleys. But such topics were of little interest to Jimmy. He steered the conversation back to a discussion of his day's work and he talked about how hard he worked. They

Jean-Marie Cueff stringing onions.

would get up at five o'clock in the morning, and would be out on the road by eight. By about four they would be back in their shop stringing onions which they would continue until 5.30 p.m. when they would go out for a few pints. Then they would continue stringing onions until 8.00 p.m. when they would have supper and a few more beers before going to bed early. It's now 6.00 p.m. and well past their time for a drink. I asked if I could go with them. ''No, we're going on our own. We don't want other people interfering. We like to keep to ourselves'' said Jimmy. Then he relented slightly ''Perhaps you can come another time. Kenavo''.

*   *   *

The next time I called to see them was less than a week later, on Tuesday, September 27. The two were preparing to go out for their early evening pint. ''May I come with you tonight?'' I asked. They were quite willing in a matter of fact way – no insincere gushing welcome. There is a mere 50 yards from their base to the Custom House – a fairly shabby old pub belonging to Brain's, Cardiff's only independent brewery. A splendid collection of beer-mats adorns one of the walls, a television set is placed over the bar door, it could do with a little paint, but it's a cheerful enough place. A collection of old-fashioned drinking glasses provide some extra character behind the bar. This was obviously their local. By the time we arrived at the bar the barman had already pulled two pints, a pint of light for Jimmy and a pint of dark for Olivier. Like true Cardiffians they referred to their beers as 'dark' and 'light' rather than 'mild' and 'bitter' although Jimmy drank Brain's Tudor light, a keg beer, not the 'real' bitter. One could occasionally find public-houses in Cardiff working class areas which did not sell the 'light' or bitter beer. The two Johnnies were evidently very appreciative of their beer – after all they had had many years to get accustomed to its taste, although Jimmy insisted that he had been a teetotaller until he was thirty.

In fact they praised the beer enthusiastically while showing themselves equally critical of the German and French beers they were 'forced' to drink at home in Brittany – that is, when they deviated from wine. ''I am drinking too much now'' says

37

Jimmy. "I will drink wine all day when I am at home, if I'm left alone. It's good for me to come to Cardiff – to drink less". He held his pint up, steady in his grip. "When I am at home, my hand would be shaking and I would spill half that beer" he said.

Olivier had put his Breton "sabots" (clogs) on his feet to walk to the Custom House and he had shuffled them very wearily on his way to the pub. He says that he walks more than Jimmy and his favourite method of hawking his onions is the time-honoured one of loading his bicycle with a huge pile of strings and wheeling it through the streets of Cardiff. Jimmy is more adventurous and he will hire a car to take him to places where the sale will be larger and quicker – valley pubs, restaurants, shops etc. "I sold 70 strings on one street corner yesterday in about fifteen minutes" says Jimmy. At a pound a string that would have been pretty good going. Neither knocks on doors these days; their customers are quite happy to run down the street after them or knock on their windows when they see an onion-seller going by. They hardly ever find it necessary to haggle over the price of a string of onions these days, it's £1 for a string, take it or leave it. "I remember selling them for one and six a string and often getting beaten down to half that price, to 9d a string" says Jimmy. Their last crop of onions has been very good, the weather had been favourable and there was more flesh to the onions than usual. The summer of 1976 had been very dry and the onions were small.

Our conversation changed to talk about the old days. Olivier talked about his first trip in 1925 when he came on a sailing ship from Roscoff to Cardiff. The ship sailed up almost to the door of the Custom House via the West Bute Dock, which has since been filled in and dried, and it was in a warehouse in Collingdon Road, a short street running parallel to Bute Street that they kept their onions, and indeed, lived.

Sometimes, ten or twelve men would sleep on the knobbly sacks of onions in the warehouse which had its back wall on the edge of the old West Bute Dock. The ship which had brought them over would then return with a load of coal. With the wind behind them the sailing ships would make the crossing in 26 hours but if the weather was unfavourable the journey could take anything up to five days. Jimmy recalled that he had once crossed on a ship which had taken nine days due to a dead calm and thick fog. These were small ships carrying around a 100 tons of onions. Sometimes they would sail in a ship owned by a man called Kervizec from Perros Guirrec but more usually they sailed directly from Roscoff to Cardiff. They talked about men called Butt and Morson who used to look after the interests of the Bretons while they were in Cardiff – organizing banking facilities and the exchange of money; but they were not always happy that they had received the best assistance possible from the two "transitaires". However, it did not take either of them long to discover how to make their own arrangements.

Jimmy had come over on his first trip in 1919 when he was nine years old. "I slept on rougher floors than this hundreds of times" he says, staring at the black linoleum floor of the Custom House. (In very different surroundings almost a year later he told me what he had been paid for that first trip. We were sitting in a cafe in St Pol de Leon when he suddenly said: "do you know what my wages were for my first season? Thirty francs, a year's rent for my mother, and a pair of boots"). "I didn't have a word of English" he admitted, "I could speak French, well, a little French anyhow. But my mother could speak nothing but Breton. She would take in washing – and wash it in the river. I have no idea who my father was – for all I know I had two or three of them". It was no small matter to start supporting his unmarried mother at the age of nine.

He talked about the welcome he had always received in Wales. The only bitter experience he could recall was when some of the valleys people tried to steal his onions in 1926, the year of the great strike, and he was only 15 years of age. In those days they would carry the onions on their backs by means of a stick called *ar vaz*. "Yes, they were bad days" recalled Jimmy. "People would take the clothes off your back if you weren't very careful". He could certainly claim that people had tried to steal the onions off his back. Nevertheless Jimmy Cueff was philosophical about his experiences. "I must admit there has always been more good than evil around, even in those bad days". And there was no suggestion that any anger survived in Jimmy from his 1926 experiences.

GJO—D

He is a plain speaker, outspoken, but it's easy to warm to him. He insists that he will not come over next year but it's not easy to believe that he will keep his word. He has been telling the same story to Cardiff journalists for at least five years but come the following September he has always been back tramping the same familiar streets. "I would be quite happy to come over without any onions to sell" he said, suggesting that he did this work because of the pleasure he received himself and gave to his buyers. It's evident that the town of Brynmawr on the Gwent-Brecon border is close to his heart. Brynmawr was his base for over half a century and it was comparatively recently that he started operating from Cardiff, with Bertevas as his partner. But he still continues to visit Brynmawr with occasional carloads of onions. "My name and address has been in the Brynmawr police station for nearly 60 years and I still return to sell in these same places".

By now Jimmy and Olivier have retired from their daily work in Brittany as farm labourers around St Pol. They buy their onions directly from farmers or occasionally from local traders and bring them over to Cardiff to sell. They therefore undertake themselves a fairly complex process of buying, exporting and retailing their onions. They hired a lorry in Brittany which came over with them on one of the ships of Brittany Ferries – the ship was the *Prince de Cornouaille* and the lorry came from Plouescat. Afterwards there is the matter of hiring cars to take the onions out into the valleys, not forgetting Jimmy's beloved Brynmawr. But Olivier never uses a car; his method is to push his heavily laden bicycle through the Cardiff streets or simply loiter on street corners or outside the Cardiff indoor market.

"Between the wars 1,400 Johnnies came over every year to England" said Jimmy. (He often talks about coming to England even when referring to Brynmawr). "By now only twenty are coming over". He gave the figure with great certainty but I think it was a very rough estimate. In the Autumn of 1968 about 40 Johnnies had taken out their licences to come over to Britain to sell onions, according to the *Association des vendeurs d'oignons* although the number was slightly less for the year referred to by Jimmy. He added "No one is going to Swansea to sell onions in Llanelli and Swansea Valley. There is no one going to

Newcastle Emlyn or sailing to Porthmadog". At that time there was one other onion seller coming over to Port Talbot, within reasonable proximity of the two in Cardiff, but Jimmy and Olivier appeared unaware of his existence. Porthmadog on the northern part of Cardigan Bay had been an important centre for the Johnnies and I have heard it said that many people in that almost totally Welsh speaking town had learnt Breton because of the large numbers of Johnnies who came annually to string their onions from their centres on the quayside and in Tremadoc. No doubt it is one of the many unsubstantiated myths which grew around the Johnnies over the years although the sight of them stringing their onions on the quay in Porthmadog on warm evenings in August and September was not uncommon.

Olivier said that he had crossed a few times from Roscoff to Swansea, ten or twelve years previously. He talked about an onion seller who made the same crossing with him but would then proceed to Newcastle Emlyn from where he would sell his onions around the farms of Dyfed.

"I don't know how he worked but he certainly sold a lot of onions" said Olivier. "He could speak Welsh very fluently but he didn't know much English. When he would be going through customs he would get me to translate for him. I think that he used to stay on a farm near Newcastle Emlyn". (Later when I went to Brittany to look for more Johnnies to interview I eventually found the Johnny who used to go to Newcastle Emlyn). Olivier told me that there were two onions sellers in Bristol at the time as well as "two youngsters" aged 40 and 45(!) selling in London. Shortly after that, in January 1978, one of the Bristol Johnnies, Eugene Cabioc'h, aged 68, disappeared on his way back to his base. To the best of my knowledge no one knows what became of him. Nevertheless, his companion, Guillaume Seite, came over as usual the following September.

It's a dying trade. "And yet" says Jimmy "the work is much easier now than it was in the old days and the money comes in fairly easily". He mentioned his son, a plumber. "The young lads these days don't want to know about hard work and they don't want to leave their wives either. Most of them prefer to sit

41

on their arses drawing dole than doing an honest day's work" claims Jimmy. We had another round and by the time we had drunk our pints it was time for them to depart. It was already getting on for 7.00 p.m. and in another hour they would be out for another pint. But as neither had been very far from his base that day they had both been back early and had strung a lot of onions in the late afternoon; so they did not intend doing much more work that night. "Come again" said Jimmy. "What about mid-day on Wednesday or Sunday? We never go selling on those afternoons. We can go on drinking for the best part of the afternoon".

I visited them again two nights later, on Thursday, September 29. When I knocked there was no reply. I looked through the hole where once there had been a lock but there was no sign of life. But as the padlock was not on the door I turned the knob and pushed.

The door opened and I called to find if there was anyone inside. There was a noise from upstairs and Jimmy shuffled wearily downstairs. "Me zo skuiz (I'm tired)", he said in Breton. I apologized and said I would call again. He nodded, but kept on talking and I followed him into the back room of the old shop. He picked up a brush and started sweeping bits of dry onion skins which had flaked away and covered the floor. He then took hold of a few rushes and started stringing, like a housewife picking up her knitting instinctively, while continuing to talk. He was obviously very tired and he talked slowly in Breton. He had been in Cardiff market and had only just returned. Olivier was still out selling. "I left my unsold onions with Olivier" he explained. "I was just too tired". "Where's Olivier now?" I asked. "I don't know, I'm not his father. No, to be honest, I have an idea where he is" replied Jimmy. "He's sure to be back before long. He hasn't eaten since ten this morning".

The sacks of onions had decreased considerably since my first visit and it was obvious they had been stringing very diligently since there were two wide rows of strings one in each room. They were laid in neat rows, width-wise on top of each other. Olivier came in pushing his bicycle, a fairly new one by all appearances, with two pieces of wood to keep the onions out of the front wheel. "I once had a bike stolen from me" he said. "It had a lot of onions on it, too, and a coat and oilskin trousers. I never got them back although I informed the police. All they found were the two bits of wood which I used to keep the onions out of the wheel".

Jimmy invited me to try and do a string myself but it was a pretty untidy effort. Nevertheless it gave me a better idea of how it is done. Six or seven single rushes, a long piece of raffia and then pick a large onion. This is attached to the rushes by winding the raffia around them and the withered stem or 'tail' of the onion.

Then, still using the same length of raffia, he attached more onions, starting with small ones and then bigger ones as one gets towards the top. The process is repeated to make another string, the two strings being then tied together to make a *pakat* or *bunch* or simply a "pound's worth" as Jimmy would say. He tied four or five *bunches* in almost as many minutes. He then said that he had recently telephoned Roscoff with a view of getting another load of onions over. "We shall have to pay for them almost immediately" he said. "You don't get long term credit in this business". Olivier had been trying to arrange for a lorry from Rumney, Cardiff to go to Roscoff to fetch the onions but if they were going to use that particular company then they would have to pay in advance.

They talked about the 1930's when both set up in business on their own. "We had to pay for the onions before we started on our journey. You would get no credit from the farmers in those days" said Olivier. He was continuing a family tradition, both his father and grandfather had been onion merchants. But Jimmy had no such tradition to follow. He simply worked very hard on the farms during the Spring and Summer in order to raise the capital needed to buy onions for his Autumn and Winter work as a Johnny. "I would not buy a steak today so that I could buy more tomorrow", he said. Living frugally in order to build up the capital to buy onions, with the profits of this year going to buy next year's onions.

Jimmy came to Wales for the first time in 1919 under the wing of a friend's father – he was then nine years of age. He was given permission to be absent from school easily enough as he would learn English and that would be an important contribution to his education. Both Jimmy and Olivier knew a man from Plougoulm, Jean-Marie Marrec, who as a child came over with his father and used to attend a school in Cardiff's dockland. "He never came after his father's retirement" said Olivier "but he can still speak English better than either of us".

Brynmawr had been Jimmy's base until he went into partnership with Olivier in 1972. But Cardiff had been Olivier's patch since his first visit at the age of 14. And it is around Cardiff that he sells nearly all his onions. "Sometimes I would take my bike loaded with onions up the valleys by train, but not often" he recalled. But Jimmy finds it difficult to keep away from his beloved Brynmawr. "Tomorrow I shall be hiring a car to take me to Bargoed, Ystrad Mynach and Caerphilly" he said. "It costs me £3 a hour and the cost of petrol but it's worth the price". The previous day he had, he claimed, banked £100 which was the result of two or three days work. He had also paid some expenses from his earnings before banking the £100.

It was time for a walk over to the Custom House and we talked about their war experiences. Both had been taken prisoners in 1940 near the border between France and Belgium and their next five years were spent in prisoner of war camps. Olivier had been imprisoned in Leipzig and Jimmy in Austria where he worked on a farm. It sounded as if Jimmy had had a pretty acceptable time there, indeed he was almost praising his life as a prisoner of war. There was no shortage of food and he would even make his own wine. "I would take a drop before breakfast even and I was 29 pounds heavier at the end of the war than I had been at the beginning" he said. As well as all that, there was a woman who wanted him to stay in Austria and marry her but he refused as he already had a wife in Brittany.

Olivier had not been quite so satisfied with his lot. He had to work for a period in a factory making springs and parts for guns in Germany. "The heat was terrible, unbearable – we only wore shorts" he recalled. But later he was transferred to a farm where he had been much happier. There had been no point in attempting to escape according to Olivier. Some of his fellow prisoners had tried but they had all been caught eventually and anyway had he managed to get home to Brittany, the Germans were there, too.

He would have had to face up to a long period of being on the run in his own country at a considerable risk to his life. Also he was 29 when the war started and by then he was probably less adventurous than he might have been. By the time he had been released he was 34 and shortly afterwards he married.

Olivier returned to Cardiff for the first time since the war in 1951 with a friend. That man died in St David's Hospital, Cardiff two years later in 1953. He had been suffering badly from blood pressure, according to Olivier. Olivier's wife and the wife of the other Johnny arrived in Cardiff a short time before he died. "His wife was anxious to take his body back to be buried in Brittany, but we could not arrange it" said Olivier. "I went back to Brittany with the two women after the burial. I had two tons of onions left unsold but I sold one ton to a Johnny in Maesteg and the rest to another Cardiff Johnny". From 1954 until 1973 Olivier's partner had been his brother in law, Vincent Cabioch. Cabioch was killed in January 1973 when he was embarking on a Brittany Ferries boat in Roscoff. He slipped on the boarding plank and fell on to the rocks below. For the past five years his "butty" had been Jimmy.

Olivier had sold onions throughout his working life in Cardiff and had only on rare occasions ventured out into the neighbouring towns and villages. "I enjoy selling onions when people are driving home from work" he said. "People are quite prepared to stop and buy a bunch or two from me".

Again our conversation had been a long one and it was seven o'clock by the time we left the bar of the Custom House. Olivier and Jimmy were going to work for two more hours before going out for another two pints in the Glendower. Bed-time would be before ten.

*   *   *

On my way to their condemned shop on Tuesday, October 4, I decided to look in the Custom House bar in case either of the Johnnies might already be there.

45

And indeed, Jimmy was there on his own drinking a pint of the dark beer. I asked him why he was not drinking his usual light. "I don't like the light in this pub" he said. "The light in the Glendower is fine – I told the barman here and he poured me a pint of this, on the house. To be honest, I quite like it". I tried to explain to him what the difference was between a keg beer and the "real" light they sold in the Glendower. But the onion-seller is very much a creature of habit and the Custom House had always been their "5.30 pub" and Jimmy and Oliver would not change that even if they preferred the beer elsewhere.

I asked about Oliver. "He hasn't finished yet" he answered. "He won't come back until he has sold every string". He added that Oliver was not feeling very well. "He works too hard". Jimmy, too, looked tired but he was obviously pleased to see me and to talk. We started talking about Breton folk tales and I asked if he was familiar with the story of Ker Ys. Not only did he know the story but he started singing extracts from the ballad:

> Bezet milliget ar verc'h wenn
> A zialc'houezaz, goude koen,
> Gore puns Ker Is, mor tremen!

(A curse on the girl who opened, after the feast, the flood-gates of Ker Ys, the sea's barrier). I asked whether he had sung the version from the *Barzaz Breiz* but he could not tell me. His eyes brightened and his face lit up with a look of happy nostalgia. He started relating the ballad, he forgot the words, then he would remember another stanza, and in fits and starts he recited most of the long ballad. "They're all drowned down here" he said, putting his hand on his heart. "But they do come to the surface now and again. They are a part of me". I asked him where he had learnt the ballad. His mother used to sing it to him when he was a child. "And while stringing the onions in the days when we were large companies we would sing the old Breton songs of our homeland". Then he started singing again, this time a snippet from a Breton ballad about the sinking of the *Titanic*:

> Ar Teitanig a zo brazad
> Lez betek breman

46

Breton onion sellers

A-vanke n'en tra varnizi
Plas da'r c'hoari a da'r bourmen.
(The Titanic is a larger vessel than any now, in no way can it be thought deficient, a place for play and dance).

"I don't care for the new songs which blare out of these transistors" he added. Then he started telling me about a ship called the *Hilda* which sank with terrible consequences to the area of the Johnnies. He knew very little about the disaster except that the ship sank near St Malo and that many onion sellers lost their lives. He believed the ship had sailed from Cardiff but he had no idea when it happened, "I think it was a long time before I was born". He knew that many had been drowned and a lot of money had gone to the bottom of the ocean causing much hardship to the area. I asked whether he knew of any ballads about the wrecking of the *Hilda* but he did not. His knowledge of what happened in the wrecking of the *Hilda* in 1905 was extremely vague but it was enough to set me on a trail which was to provide me with material for the chapter on "Disasters" in this book.

He then began talking about other ships, *L'Herman* and *L'Oceanie* which used to sail from Roscoff to Cardiff before returning to Brittany loaded with Welsh coal. "I remember how we would sail up the West Bute Dock, unload the onions from the ship straight onto a train which would take us up the valleys to Brynmawr". Then Olivier arrived.

His face had a bluish-grey colour, he looked exhausted, frail and rather pitiful. But after a few mouthfulls of his beer and a few minutes talk in the pub's comfortable warmth he looked much better. He had had a hard day. He had been out to Llandaff, some four miles from his base and had taken a round-about route on his way back. "I stayed for a while under the Gabalfa fly-over – it's a good place to sell when people are driving home from work, and it's dry" he said.

He had also been to Rhiwbina and met a 'Protestant Padre' while he was pushing his bicycle through the streets. That same person had bought many strings from Olivier the previous year and had made the onion-seller promise to call the next time he was over. "But I did not call" said Olivier. "I never knock on doors these days. But I was happy to have seen him and we had

48

a long conversation". "Protestant or Catholic" commented Jimmy, "I couldn't care less, as long as I get their money". Jimmy likes to give the impression of being a secular character, a keen bargainer, but Olivier is an altogether tougher person. Olivier said that he never knocked on doors but he called in restaurants and shops. He had called earlier that day in a wine shop in North Road and sold a number of strings to the proprietor, who was an old friend of Olivier's. They had a few glasses of wine, too, before the onion-seller departed.

Jimmy said that his day had been a hard one too. He had been outside Cardiff market all day and sales had been rather slow. Nevertheless he was happy with the way the season was going. The previous day he had arranged the transfer of £1,700 from his Cardiff bank to his bank in Brittany. "Your wife will be pleased" I ventured. He replied that his wife did not ask anything from him. She would be happier to have him at home – she, also, is drawing her pension. Jimmy mentioned his grandsons, one was 16 and the other 12. The elder had had trouble with his school examinations and would have to re-sit them the following year, adding with a little pride that he gave some assistance towards the children's education.

I enquired about his plans to bring over another load of onions. "We shall certainly be getting more onions" said Jimmy. "The crop has been very good and the onions are first class. I think we will be in Cardiff for Christmas this year, the first time for five years that we will not be home for Christmas. Last year we were home in Brittany very early, we had sold the lot, and had we wanted to bring over another load the onions were very poor. The summer was very dry and the onions were small and they didn't have much of a 'tail' either so they were hard to string".

Once he and Olivier had sold off their present stock they would return to Roscoff for a week before returning with a fresh supply. They had already paid all the rent due for the shop to the end of the season so there would be no more deductions in that direction.

Jimmy turned the conversation towards one of his favourite subjects – the old days in Brynmawr. At one time he would hire a horse and cart to take his onions around the neighbouring villages. On one occasion he and his partner were returning home around midnight when someone came stealthily up behind them and stole one of the sticks they used to carry onions on their shoulder. With the stick that person hit another man who was walking on the road. "I thought that he'd been killed" said Jimmy. "We went away as fast as we could. The man must have been alright, though, because we didn't hear anything about anyone being killed". It was the uncertainty of a man in a strange situation in a strange country.

Olivier said that at one time he had a hand-cart which he pushed around the streets of Cardiff until he discovered that people would steal the occasional string from the cart. He would leave his loaded hand-cart on a street corner and with his "ar vaz" carry a few strings from house to house. After selling them he would return to his hand-cart for more. Unfortunately, some people took advantage of the unguarded cart and helped themselves to the onions. The bicycle later proved a better implement of transport as he could keep it close to him at all times and he could ride it back to his base after selling all the onions. It seems that some onion-sellers had made a fine art of loading their bicycles so that they could ride it even when it was fully laden as well (see pictures of Claude Deridon in Porthmadoc).

We said our merry farewells to the Custom House regulars and I received another pressing invitation to join them for a lunchtime drink at the Glendower the following Sunday.

I went to the shop again on Friday, October 7 but that evening the padlock was on the door. I looked into the bar of the Custom House but they were not there either. I wondered whether one of them might be ill. Olivier had certainly looked drawn and very tired earlier in the week. But on the following morning, doing the Saturday shopping in Cardiff, I saw Olivier pushing his bicycle towards the centre of the city, but later when I went to talk to him he had gone. Jimmy, however, was in his usual Saturday place by the entrance to the market. He was sitting on the concrete edge of a large rubbish bin with his bicycle beside him. He made no effort at all to sell his onions, just waiting there patiently for the customers to come to him. We talked briefly – he had been to Brynmawr the previous day

Olivier Bertevas with his bike and onions in the centre of Cardiff.

and Olivier had also had a long day. That morning in Cardiff the onions were selling quickly and Olivier had gone to get some more.

*   *   *

The Sunday lunch-time rendezvous of the two onion-sellers was the Glendower. In the side-streets of that part of Cardiff most of the houses were empty with the windows and doors bricked up. One house, which was still inhabitied, had a poster in the window protesting about empty houses and a shortage of homes. The houses have all been demolished by now. At 12.30 p.m. life was in full swing in the bar – darts, dominoes, cards, and a lot of joking and leg-pulling. Someone was telling a story about a newcomer to a card school who had lost a packet the night before. Jimmy was at the bar and had just bought a bottle of wine and two pints. He offered to buy me a pint and then realised he did not have enough money. He went to borrow some from Olivier but by the time he returned I had been served and paid for my drink. He seemed genuinely cross with me so I apologized and promised he could buy me a pint later.

The Glendower has as rich a racial mix as any pub in Cardiff's dockland, with more coloured people than white although everyone speaks the same flat "Ci-a-a-diff accent". There were no women in the bar, whether they were not admitted there or were all home preparing Sunday dinner I did not discover.

The Glendower certainly appeared a potentially rougher pub than the Custom House. Whatever opinions the two Johnnies might have had about the pub they were unanimous in their praise of the beer, Olivier with his dark and Jimmy his (real) light. Both were obviously well-known in the pub. A witty character, youngish but with a middle-age spread and dark hair carefully plastered into place asked Jimmy: "Got any garlic for me?". "You buying a pint?" replied Jimmy. "No comprende pint" said the wit. "No comprende garlic, either" said Jimmy, equal to the banter.

Someone left and I found space to sit next to Olivier. Had I possessed the artist's talent to sketch their faces from memory it would have been much easier to draw Olivier than Jimmy. He is much the quieter person but he is readier to speak freely about his experiences and his memories, and to contribute all he knows. It is probable that he has a better idea than Jimmy of what I want and what interests me. He is a small man with a gentle face and a ready smile. There is an odd lateral dent to his nose as if he had been caught by an ill-directed right cross. Jimmy is a rougher character, likes to talk expansively but is certainly not as interesting as Olivier. Anything he offers as fact has to be carefully checked. Jimmy appeared particularly scruffy that day, he had not shaved for about four or five days, but Olivier looked much tidier although he was still wearing clogs. But they were not his usual clogs, these were stained brown, presumably his Sunday best clogs! Jimmy was talking to an incredibly well-dressed man about the war years.

Olivier talked about his father who had paid his last visit to Cardiff in 1939 – he had been over 55 times previously. He lived to see Olivier return safely from the war and enjoyed a few more years of his son's company. Olivier, however, could recall little of what his father had told him of his experiences as an onion-seller. Olivier then spoke of life in a warehouse in Collingdon Road when the Johnnies slept on the floor or even on top of the sacks of onions. There was a fire-place in the warehouse and they would exchange onions for lumps of coal when the weather was cold.

The previous season, 1976, they had a house in Adamsdown, a house which had been demolished before their 1977 visit. "The difficulty with a house" said Olivier "is that it has a lot of rooms and they are all small. The place we have this year is much better. We can keep all our onions in one room". The front room of a shop could accommodate their entire stock of onions. His one complaint about the shop was that he had to go down two floors to the cellar and then out to the back in order to go to the toilet.

We then discussed more uplifting subjects. They never went to church on Sundays, now. Evidently it was not as easy to remain good Catholics in Cardiff as in St Pol de Leon; at least their wives were there to keep an eye on them. And anyway who wants to go to church and find people turning up their noses at him because he stinks of onions and garlic? After a week's hard slog and loitering, frozen on street corners it is too great a temptation to spend Sunday in the warmth and quiet trying to ease some of their weariness. But even on a Sunday they still get up at 6.00 a.m. to string more onions. The main difference between Sunday and another day was that they did not go out selling. "We mustn't take it easy" said Olivier, "We will always have plenty of onions to sell on Monday, all strung and ready, but what about Tuesday? We've got to keep on with the work". So they keep on with the work until just before midday and then it's over to the Glendower for opening time. In the old days they would go to church every Sunday morning but as Olivier said, how does one compare the Cardiff Catholic churches with the Cathedral in St Pol de Leon, or the "Kreisker" or the splendidly gilded Notre-Dame de Croaz-Baz in Roscoff? The only occasion he would go to church in Cardiff now would be on All Saints' Day, to pay their respects to the dead. Jimmy, at last, came over to join us.

"On All Saints Day we will be remembering our parents and forefathers" he said. It looked as if they would be home in Brittany for All Saints Day and the thought appeared to please him.

"But even if we were in Cardiff we would go to the church and we wouldn't work for the rest of the day. We would spend the rest of the day in a pub although it's not the best way to remember your parents. When we're home in Brittany the women make sure that we go to church although we go to the café for a drop of wine". He hinted that he hoped his son in turn would remember him on All Saints day.

"We never work on Sunday when we're home in Brittany" added Olivier. "We go to Mass in the morning then to the café for a chat and a glass of wine on our way home, a large dinner and then we play *boules* all afternoon". A day of rest and recreation, very different to the everyday life of a Johnny Onions in Cardiff. Olivier said that Jimmy had once been on a pilrimage to Lourdes. "I would like to go there myself" he said, "but only for a week-end. I would like to be there on a Sunday. I wouldn't like to go on a week's excursion as Jimmy did. It's a funny thing" he added, "but a man was talking on the radio this morning telling how he had had a miraculous cure at

54

The Cathedral of St. Pol de Leon.

Lourdes". He was born, it seemed, dumb, but after visiting Lourdes he was able to speak perfectly and he was there on the radio, audible proof of the miracle. Neither Jimmy nor Olivier could tell me for certain to which service they were listening – they thought it was the Radio Luxembourg French service.

Jimmy recalled his visit to Lourdes and the surprise he had on hearing someone on the train singing, in Breton the ballad *Itroun Varia Rumengol* (Our Lady of Rumengol). It immediately brought to mind Anatole Le Braz in his *Au Pays des Pardons* recalling a journey he made by train to the Rumengol Pardon. Suddenly a young soldier sitting opposite Le Braz got up and sang in a lovely voice that very song:

> Lili, arc'hantet ho delliou,
> War vord an dour 'zo er prajou;
> Doue d'ezho roas dillad
> A skuill er meziou peb c'houez vad...

(The lilies with their silver leaves border the streams in the meadows; God gave them clothes to spread their sweet scents over the fields).

"If I went again I would be better prepared for the journey" said Jimmy, ever practical in his approach. "I took a bag of sandwiches with me on my way to Lourdes but I didn't know that the train did not stop and I shared them with a stranger. For the return journey I was better prepared but on that occasion I bought too much food and it was all dried up in the warm fine weather".

We then talked about the 'pilgrimages', the Breton *pardons.* Olivier said that he had been once to the pardon at Rumengol. This is the *Pardon of the Singers,* where the singers of ballads from bygone days would come to worship and sing their songs. "I went there by car some years after the war" said Oliver. "My brother wanted to go there some years later and to walk all the way, but I said that the only way I would go would be on my bike. I am not that fond of walking".

Olivier regretted that the St Pol *pardon* was no longer observed. "The new priest had no interest in the custom. I remember how we would go from house to house collecting wood for the bonfire. Gosh, we had a lot of fun in those days" he said. He added that the priest in Roscoff had made a lot of restrictions to the fun of that town's *pardon* too. "He won't permit the celebrations to continue over into the following Monday. The young people don't have the same interest in the old customs".

We turned to discussing the subject of playing cards and dominoes for money, which was going on all around us. "Someone knocked on our door the other night and said that he had come for a game" said Olivier. "I said he was welcome to have a game, but we would be playing with onions, not money. Somebody must have been using the shop as a card-school before we started using it. We never play with anyone. In Brittany, it's different, I will enjoy a game, in a café – dominoes usually.

If I win, you buy me a drink; if you win, I buy you a drink. But here in Cardiff, I have seen people betting, a pound or more a go, a pound becomes a fiver or a tenner and some poor creature goes home without his pay-packet".

It is evident that the two are careful to keep well clear of the temptations of gambling; very wise when one considers the large sums of money they might have with them after a good day's selling. One of them said that they had about three weeks selling left, sales had dropped a little recently. Their intention was to go home and to stay there for two weeks before returning with another load of onions. But were they as enthusiastic as they had been a fortnight previously? They wanted to be sure of the price of onions in Brittany before coming back, but I had the feeling that they would return. Olivier talked about his efforts to persuade his younger brother over to sell onions. "He is a strong boy, and young; he's only 55" said Olivier. "But he worries over the language difficulty; he speaks no English. I had to learn English when I was going about my work and I don't see why he couldn't do the same". But he had to admit that one cannot expect a middle-aged person to learn another language as easily as a youngster. "After all, I didn't come over during the war years and when I came again it was quite difficult at first. But I will never forget my English again". As well as the language problem, he added that his brother was doing rather too well with his vegetable stall in the market at St Pol.

Olivier rolled himself another cigarette and offered his

tobacco box. I said, apologetically, that I would not object to trying to roll a neat cigarette after a lapse of many years but I suspected his strong shag would do my lungs no good at all. Even in Brittany where cigarettes are very cheap, the Johnnies still roll their own cigarettes. Then their saliva, as they hardly ever take their cigarettes from their lips, mixes with the nicotine juice turning the paper to a nasty, sickly brown. But to those who spend their lives in the open air, perhaps the habit is not as injurous to health as one might expect.

He started discussing one of this favourite topics – beer. "This beer is not what it used to be" claimed Olivier. "The Kronenberg in Brittany is very strong but it doesn't taste as good as this stuff. I'll have a pint or a half of the local brew when I'm passing through Plymouth but there's no beer like *Brains*. But it's not as strong as it used to be. In the old days three pints would have put any one of us flat on our backs". By now they had both drunk three pints and I, who had started participating rather later than they had, drunk two and a half pints – and we were all in judge-like condition.

It was then time for the Sunday dinner, something of an occasion. The local butcher cooked it for them and on their way from the Glendower they called at his house to collect the meal which they carried back to their base with the utmost care and respect. Together with the bottle of wine purchased by Jimmy they would have a lunch which would enable them to face another week of warmed-up potage. After eating they would settle down to write a letter to let people at home know "that we're still alive". They would aim to catch the 5.00 p.m. collection, even though there was no collection between mid-day on Saturday and Monday morning. But I said nothing. It seemed that they had noticed the changes in the Post Office's arrangements since they last came to Cardiff. Anyway, why should I upset the habits of decades. "We also get letters by return" said Jimmy. I left them hungry for their dinner and looking forward to the weekly ritual of writing home.

When I arrived at the shop on Tuesday, October 11, Jimmy was there alone, casually stringing his onions. There was only a very small pile of onions already strung but that did not worry him as he would be spending most of the following day doing that work – that was the order of things. I asked him about growing onions. "There are no machines to sow or harvest onions" he said.

"All the work must be done by hand. More often than not these days I buy my onions from merchants who have bought them from the farmers. Sometimes I buy them directly from the farmers which saves me having to pay commission to the merchants, but it's far less trouble for me to buy from a merchant".

He had spent that day selling onions around Cardiff, but it had been a poor day; he had only sold £25 worth. I asked him how much a string weighed. Somewhere between four and five pounds he replied and then stressing rather defensively that he sold his onions by the string and not by the pound. He repeated his statement more than once as if my question implied some criticism of the methods of the Johnnies.

He began telling a story about a lorry-load of onions which the previous year had arrived a day earlier than expected. "We had been told that he would be coming on Wednesday but he arrived at lunch-time on Tuesday. We were both out, up the mountain getting a load of reeds and when we got home late in the afternoon there waiting for us was a large load of onions and a very tired driver who had been waiting for hours". The two of them were also very tired, so they went over to the pub and got a crowd of unemployed men, who for £5 an hour, unloaded the onions. Jimmy explained that nowadays he would always get some men from the pub or the employment exchange if he wanted to move a load of onions. "I never put a hundredweight sack of onions on my back now, but Olivier will carry them with the best. I remember one Johnny years ago who could carry two sackfuls, each weighing a hundredweight across his shoulders, one on top of the other. In ten journeys that man could move a ton of onions. It was the kind of feat much appreciated by Olivier, but Jimmy was disdainful of such herculean efforts, particularly as he would no longer attempt to carry heavy loads on his back.

I asked him about getting the reeds. He showed a huge bread knife he used for cutting the reeds; it was not surprising that he considered the work tedious and tiring. "Would you like a

59

piece of *kouign avalou* (apple tart)?" he asked. I accepted happily and he took an apple tart out of a filthy cupboard which I had not previously noticed and proceeded to cut it using the knife he used for cutting the reeds. It was an excellent tart, obviously home-made, but he did not say where it had come from. "Mind you, this stringing is bloody hard work" he said suddenly. "Hard on the arms and shoulders?" I asked. "No, on the feet" he replied. "We have to stand hour after hour, round shouldered, stringing endlessly". It was not surprising that Jimmy's shoulders and back had grown stiff and rounded after years of standing in that position.

He started talking about his normal day's work. "We get up about 5.30 a.m., fry some bacon and eggs or boil an egg each, with bread and butter, of course. I often have bacon and egg for breakfast when I am home in Brittany – these habits become a part of you. We might have a stew for dinner if we're here , and our home-made soup, or potage, for supper every night. I make up the potage on a Sunday and warm it up every night for the rest of the week. Now and again, we get something better, a steak or rabbit. Unfortunately, we haven't got an oven, so we have to ask the butcher to roast our Sunday joint for us. I'm afraid Olivier will have to make do with sausages tonight".

He was particularly free and forthcoming with information as we talked that night. He said that the weekly rent on the old shop was £4 and that the building was condemned. He added that he and Olivier had to pay £6 a ton import duty on all the onions they brought into Britain and that he had to get a licence from the *Association des vendeurs d'oignons de Roscoff et de sa région*. "Sometimes a young policeman will ask me if I have a licence to sell onions here" he said. "I tell him straight that I had a licence to sell onions here long before he was born".

While he is stringing Jimmy throws the smallest onions into a bag. "I sell them for pickling at 20p a pound". Suddenly he said that he did not like talking and working at the same time and we would go out for a pint. As I was going through the door out to the shop's passage I almost tripped over a bucket full of water. I asked whether the roof leaked. "No, but I leak" he answered. "I've got to piss somewhere and it's a long walk

60

from the loft, down to the cellar and out the back, especially at night when it's dark down the cellar".

We had long been settled comfortably in the Custom House but still Olivier had not arrived and Jimmy began showing signs of concern. When it's time to return to the shop, or "mond d'ar ger" (go home) as Jimmy says it, he does just that. But not Olivier. Olivier will not return until he has sold every string of onions. And he will not sell his onions for less than £1 a string. "When I'm tired I'll sell the last few on my bike for 90p or even 80p" says Jimmy "but Olivier never does that. They all cost a £1 from him". Olivier appears a far gentler person than the outwardly rough Jimmy but Olivier is certainly the more stubborn of the two. That night I had the feeling that if either of them would not come to Cardiff the following year it would be Jimmy and that Olivier would somehow keep coming to the very end. Olivier evidently is the tighter-fisted of the two and Jimmy is full of praise and admiration for his uncompromising diligence. "Olivier is one of the *tud kaled* (hard folk), he's a real Breton" said Jimmy. "He'd been calling me Charlie Chaplin recently and I said I would give him a hiding. If you can't call a man by his real name, you're not showing him much respect". One could hardly expect two men co-existing in these conditions to be able to avoid the occasional quarrel.

Jimmy was evidently uncomfortable at having quarrelled with Olivier and he praised his partner for his diligence and ability to get up in the morning. "I would be quite happy to lie in for a while every morning if I were left alone. If I were home with my wife I wouldn't be getting up until 9.00

"My alarm clock is broken and I can't see the time on my wrist watch in the early morning, but Olivier is sure to wake and get up on the dot at 5.30" he said. Jimmy's bark is certainly far worse than his bite – from time to time he will snap at me, telling me, not without cause, I expect, to mind my own business. His mood can change with equal rapidity, and he can just as suddenly start telling me some private or personal secret. He told me how a man had once snatched an onion from a string he had on his shoulder. "I chased him, tore the onion from his hand and then hit him in the eye with the onion – he must have had a beauty of a shiner. A man's got to defend his possessions''.

He was prepared to admit that he and Olivier often felt nervous and uncertain in Cardiff. Sometimes someone will knock on their door late at night asking for the time, "You've got to be careful or they'll take your watch off you". They do not make friends easily. In half a century Jimmy says that he never went looking for women in Cardiff. "We're both married and anyway who at our age wants to go looking for women". As Jimmy went for another pint the barman said something to him and pointing to a youngish woman playing darts in the corner he put his right hand on his bicep and flexed the muscle. The woman revealed a marvellous expanse of bosom and the deepest of cleavages. Jimmy understood the comment and the significance of the gesture but there was no smile and no gleam came to his eye. I heard that the Custom House once had the reputation for being something of a centre for girls following the "old profession".

It was nearly 7.00 by the time Olivier had arrived at the Custom House – cheerful and rather excited. When he got back to the shop he said he found a small hand-cart outside the door. He had taken it into the passage as it would be ideal to take onions around the streets. His face was alight with pleasure. "I don't know whether I will be able to wheel it along the pavements but I should be OK if I go along the street keeping close to the side" he said. "It's a pity that it isn't a little bigger but it will do very nicely".

A few days earlier there had been a story about the two Johnnies in the Cardiff morning paper, the *Western Mail*, and Olivier had profited considerably from the publicity on this day. One woman, having read their annual assurances that this would positively be their last season in Cardiff and worried that she might never see her beloved onion-man again had chased after him and bought six strings. But on the whole both had had a hard day. Most of the shops were closed for the half-day and there were very few people about. Olivier drank his pint suddenly and we went back to the shop to see the "hand-cart" which Oliver had found. It was a super-market trolley, and to Olivier's obvious disappointment, I had to advise him not to use it to carry onions through the streets of Cardiff in case he got into difficulties with the police. And so I left a disappointed Olivier and Jimmy to face another hour or two's stringing before they went to the Glendower for their night-cap.

*   *   *

The number of full sacks of onions had decreased considerably when I called a week later, on Wednesday, October 9. "We've got another fortnight's work" said Jimmy. He was there on his own and Olivier had still not returned. Jimmy was in excellent spirits and he admitted that the season was going well. The previous year they had returned to Brittany in November and had not bothered to come back to Cardiff with another load. But this had been a good year. There had been a first-class crop of onions in Brittany and the farmers just did not know what to do with them. "I will be taking these empty sacks back with me" he said. "They've cost me 20p each and I've got nearly 500 of them".

He had been back in Brynmawr that day – he goes there once a fortnight. On that day he looked unusually spruce, shaven, wearing a dark blue cardigan and a brown shirt although in his usual corduroy trousers. He was stringing onions, relaxed and contented but not totally happy that Olivier had not returned. "That's his corner and this is mine".

"I like to have him there to talk to when I'm working".

I asked whether he had been seriously ill or had an accident while in Wales. He said that a light lorry had once gone over his foot but he had not had to stay in hospital.

Olivier came back – as usual he was wearing his overalls, red pullover and black shirt. Both wear caps with short peaks. Olivier takes off his boots, puts on his slippers before slipping his feet, slippers and all, into the large clogs. "Some fresh air for the feet" he said, adding that the clogs were too large to be worn without the slippers.

The previous day the two had been to fetch rushes from the mountain side between Ystrad Mynach and Nelson, Olivier cutting them with a sickle and Jimmy with his bread knife! They had tied the reeds on top of their hired car and Olivier, eyes sparkling, described the looks on the faces of people as they

63

drove past in what appeared like a mobile hay-rick. Sometimes they would fetch a load from as far as Brynmawr. Olivier recalled that he had been getting reeds from Church Village. He, and his brother-in-law, the late Vincent Cabioch had been selling onions in that area, and in Pontypridd and Treforest. (I learnt later that the old stables behind the 'White Hart' in Pontypridd had been an important centre for the Johnnies in the years before the last war).

Jimmy described how he and one of his partners in Brynmawr used to have a vehicle of their own – an old large van. They would leave the van in the town for the rest of the year, paying £1 a month to have it kept in a garage while they were in Brittany. "Two vans saw their last days with us in Brynmawr. They were both old, second-hand vehicles anyway" he said. It was in that period that he started going out of Brynmawr to sell, travelling as far as Aberdare, Rhondda and over the Rhigos mountain to Glyn Neath.

I couldn't drive but my partner had a licence and I would contribute my share of the cost".

Olivier added that he and one of his "butties" once had a van in Cardiff but for one winter only. The old van would never start and they would beg all the men they could find to push it up and down the street, and sometimes all the pushing in the world would not get it going!

By then we were settled in expansive comfort in the bar of the Custom House and Olivier began praising the produce of Ely Brewery, an ale that once competed with that of Brains, for the honour of quenching the thrist of the discerning Cardiffian. "Wine does more harm to me than beer" claimed Jimmy. "Wine makes my hands shake". He held out his hand, steady and firm. "That's the difference between beer and wine. Back home I drink a litre a day of wine. Drinking wine with food does no harm to anyone, but drinking between meals – that's when the trouble comes".

With Jimmy saying "Ma labourez e-peus gwenneg ivez" (My work provides the pennies, also) we finished our pints and they prepared to return to work. The two noticed that I scribbled Jimmy's comment on the margin of a discarded 'Echo' and one of them asked me whether I could write Breton. I replied that I

64

once used the language to correspond with friends in Brittany. What about them? They both could, but not with ease. They always wrote in French to their wives but talked with them in Breton. "It's easier to quarrel in Breton" said Olivier with a smile.

Summer time had ended by the time I paid my next visit to the two Johnnies and as I walked towards the top end of Bute Street at about 5.45 it was already dark. I walked under the bridge and saw Olivier pushing his bicycle about 50 yards ahead of me so I followed him instead of first looking into the Custom House as I usually did.

I arrived at the door and called after him. It was almost pitch dark except for a tiny speck of light at the end of the passage. Olivier answered and called me in. He was in the back room trying to take off his wellingtons. The only light was a candle stuck into a wine bottle and in that subdued flicker the old shop had an almost presentable appearance. I helped him to take off his wellingtons and he moaned at having to wear them at all. "They're no good for the feet, but I suppose they're better than being wet" he said. He did not approve of turning the clocks back for the winter, either. "I know it's better for children going to school in the morning – it's light for them, at least. But I don't get home in the evenings now until it's dark". He put on his slippers before slipping his feet, slippers and all into his clogs. He had bought a new pair of boots recently but they had already been ruined in the rain. There was not a single sackful of onions left in the shop, only a neat pile of onions all strung and ready to sell. Their electricity supply had just been cut off. Olivier explained that a man from the Electricity board had called and discovered that the building had no meter. It was obvious that they had been supplied with electricity for which they could not be charged, so their supply was unceremoniously discontinued. He should have called that morning at 10.00 a.m. to reconnect the supply and install a meter. But the electricity man had not kept his promise and time was money for Olivier. The little Breton had left at 10.05 a.m. to sell his onions! According to the note which had been pushed under the door the electricity man had called at 10.15 and found a locked door. Olivier and Jimmy would have to make do with a candle. They used camping gas for their cooking.

When Jimmy arrived we all went to the Custom House. The transfer of money from a Cardiff bank to Britain was causing them some concern. "We have paid the money into the bank here in Cardiff but it isn't in our bank in Brittany" said Jimmy. "You're an educated chap, if I charge 20p a pound how much will I get on 12 tons? I'll tell you, I've banked nearly £5,000 on behalf of both of us, over the past five weeks.

"This week I had a letter from my wife – do you trust your wife? I do: And she says that nothing has come through to the bank in Roscoff. I've got the receipts so I must be alright, but I worry a bit. I'll have to go to the bank tomorrow, and maybe for half a day's selling, to argue with some buggers who are laughing at me". Transferring money from British banks directly to banks in Brittany was an important subject of discussion in 1950 when Mazeas asked Mareschal to discuss the possibilities with the Bank of England. There were other problems at that time, as there were restrictions on the amount of onions that could be taken into Britain. Thus, if any Johnny took more money out of Britain than the value of the onions he had initially imported he was likely to get into some trouble with the port authorities.

In the past the onion sellers would take their earnings home with them at the end of the season – not a totally safe practice but neither had had any unpleasant experiences. According to Jimmy they would conceal their money in their boots, about their persons and in their belts. That was the method they used at the time the *Hilda* was sunk when many people and much money was lost. Gradually, with the help of an agent in Cardiff and eventually by doing the work themselves they got used to making their own transferences through the banks. But even they had had some difficulties. In 1976 when returning via Folkstone they were stopped for having too much money in sterling. They thought it would have been a clever idea to take a little extra in sterling ready for the next time they would be coming over. But at the time they were restricted to taking £25 each and they had to exchange £60 each in francs before sailing. "And I'm not sure we got full value in the exchange either" said Olivier. "And as well as that the arguing caused us to miss the boat and we had to pay a second time to make the crossing".

There was very little more work to do on this trip. There were only about 80 strings left and Olivier himself had sold two bike loads during the day.

He said that he would have 40 strings of onions on his bicycle when it was fully loaded. They were both confident that they would be returning to Roscoff on the 11.00 a.m. boat on the following Saturday. "I don't like the crossing. It makes me terribly sea-sick" said Olivier.

A youngish woman wearing a recklessly low dress concealing a very ample bosom came up to us to try and sell raffle tickets in aid of the blind. Jimmy groaned a bit at being asked to contribute and she replied curtly "I don't want your money, it's for the blind". We all bought tickets and after she had gone Jimmy said "I don't like her. She slapped me once". He never told me why.

Before departing we talked a little about some Welsh poems in praise of the Johnny Onions which I had found. Both were intrigued that I should read and write Welsh. As I was not absolutely certain that they would return after their week back in Brittany I asked them for their home addresses. Both wrote their addresses laboriously in a large but pleasant hand-writing, it was not something which came easily to them – Jean-Marie Cueff, Lagat-Vran, Roscoff, Finistere and Olivier Berteras, Rue Chateaubriand, Saint Pol de Leon, Finistere. Olivier was evidently keen to come back but Jimmy at that moment did not seem to care much whether he came or not. But he seemed reasonably confident that they would both be back in a fortnight's time unless there might be some trouble over the money.

As I did not see either of them selling onions in Cardiff for some time after they had returned to Roscoff, it was Wednesday, November 23 by the time I called again in 253 Bute Street. I could see there was a light inside but the door was padlocked on the outside. I walked back to the Custom House and found Olivier there on his own. Jimmy had gone to get some reeds. Two days earlier, according to Olivier, they had been to get reeds near Ystrad Mynach but everywhere was under water and they had returned empty handed.

They had both returned to Cardiff on the previous Sunday with 14 tons of onions, they had paid around £1,300 for them as well as £400 for a lorry to bring the load over. They had had to wait a while in Bristol as the lorry was carrying some lettuce which had to be delivered there.

The onions were in excellent condition. Had been offered ten tons by one farmer alone "but their tails were short and you can't string those". So he bought two tons from that farmer and most of the remaining 12 tons from other farms. When he had returned to St Pol de Leon he was very pleased to find his daughter home on holiday from Paris with her two children, a two year old girl and a 12 month old son. "He's very dark, the boy, a real Breton" said Olivier "and he's very steady on his feet already". The family lived in a flat in Paris and both parents were working full-time.

Olivier also said that he had bought a ton and a half of onions from another Johnny who had decided not to make a second visit. That particular Johnny owned a small farm and grew his own onions.

We went back to the shop. There was a heap of coal on the floor of the front room and a scorching fire in the grate in the back room where they strung the onions. Olivier started stringing effortlessly, casually, while moaning gently that some of the onions had short tails.

Their electricity had been re-connected and in the harsh light of the bare bulb the room was a more pitiful sight than ever. A rabbit in a plastic bag hung from a nail in the door but as Jimmy, the chef, had not returned there was little hope of having it for supper that night.

There was a strong wind that night and every so often it blew open the front door with a tremendous clatter. Eventually Olivier bolted it from the inside. Some time later there was a knock on the door – Jimmy had returned with his hired car and 'chauffer'. He had a small pile of reeds but his load was mostly straw. As he came in the two argued fiercely – Olivier complaining that Jimmy had spent money on straw and Jimmy explaining in very short tempered tones that if he wanted reeds he would have to go to the top of a mountain somewhere, everywhere else was under water.

After they had finished bringing the reeds and straw into the shop, we all returned to the Custom House. Jimmy told me that the money he had been worrying about the last time we talked had been safely transferred to his bank in Brittany. The transfer had apparently taken place the day after his wife had written to him. Olivier greeted two women in the bar. "We were neighbours a few years ago when we rented a house in another street" he said.

Every time I called on them now I would find Jimmy on his own, either in the Custom House or in the shop. Monday, November 28 was no exception. He was stringing onions with a roaring fire in the grate. In fact he was worrying about cracking noises that came from the back of the fire-place. I said that I thought it was the fire-bricks expanding and that it was alright. I tried to take out one of the loose bricks to show him but then he thought he could see a fire behind the fireplace while I tried to persuade him that what he was seeing was a relection of the flames.

Since Jimmy told me what he knew of the sinking of the *Hilda* I had tried to find out more about the disaster and a few days earlier I had received some information and some pictures from Brittany. He was most interested. I had also received a list of centres from which the Johnnies had been selling onions in 1937. "It doesn't name Brynmawr" he said. "*Gast* *, I was there!".

He considered it was time to go for a pint. It was becoming more and more obvious that Jimmy was getting tired of the hard work and the cold weather. He had had a hard day selling outside the Cardiff market and he had come back without selling all his onions. "Oliver is a far better seller than me" he said. "He's good to his children, too.

"He bought a car for his daughter this year – she lives in Paris – and two years ago he bought his son a car. Both cost £2,500 at least – it's not a small matter for a labourer. He's still paying for his house – I finished paying for mine five years ago".

A little later Olivier came in, stamping his feet noisily. He looked frozen to the marrow but he'd had a good day. He had

(* Breton for prostitute – a common oath with Breton speakers)

sold two bicycle loads, a total of £80. "Thank God we split the money straight down the middle" said Jimmy. Olivier smiled. It did not seem to bother him in the least that he worked harder than Jimmy. He asked me whether he could have a copy of the picture of the *Hilda* as a relative of his grandfather was among the five who had been saved. The picture I had was a photostat copy so I gave it to him and promised that I would bring one for Jimmy next time.

Jimmy suddenly started singing, he claimed he had made up the song himself:

> J'etais depuis 1919 en Angleterre
> est j'ai fait une chanson de moi...

I saw them for the last time in Cardiff two days before Christmas. I had gone to see them, curious, and a little concerned, as to how they would be spending the day. All was well. They were going to spend Christmas day with their 'chauffeur' said Jimmy. I also wanted to buy a string of onions and for my £1 they filled my pockets as well. The onions had been selling well in the period leading up to Christmas and they had sold half their November shipment. Olivier was also pleased with the way the garlic was selling. Many people would come to him for onions and then ask him whether he also had garlic to sell. He would never ask his customers if they wanted garlic. Olivier was fairly confident that they would be home in Brittany by mid-January but he was concerned that a lot of the onions they had bought had short 'tails', which made stringing difficult. The onions with poor 'tails' would be sold by the sackful to shop-keepers but they were not buying at the moment. The floor of the shop was soaking wet. Once again they had failed to get reeds for stringing and had to buy straw and they were very annoyed with a farmer in the Bridgend area whom they claimed had charged a ridiculous sum for it.

They had a cat with them this time, a friendly and pretty ragdoll. "She's adopted me" said Jimmy. "There are plenty of mice here so it's handy to have a cat. Mind you, mice don't eat onions".

We went to the Custom House for the last time. Jimmy was obviously very tired and he kept nodding off in his chair. "It's better to keep going, you see" he said "this is no good. If I

70

relax, I drop off''. But Olivier would not sleep anywhere except on his mattress upstairs and he would be awake again at four the next morning, ready to get up at five-thirty.

The Johnnies at Home

The only explanation I have ever heard for the nick-name 'Johnny' on the onion-sellers is that so many of them had the Christian name Jean-Yves. Be that as it may, somewhere between the glorious 'Kreisker' church of St Pol de Leon, the *Rendez-vous des Amis* café in Lagat Vran and the *Bar des Johnnies* in Roscoff Jean-Marie Cueff stopped being Jimmy and became Shamar or Sham-Bar. Yan-Bar is an acceptable Breton form of Jean-Marie, thus Shamar or Sham-Bar would be a corruption drawing on elements of both French and Breton forms of the name. When I re-started my researches in September 1978, nine months after they had said their final farewells to Cardiff and Wales, my most difficult problem was to find the two of them, in spite of the fact that they had given me their addresses. Finally, after half a day's inquiring and searching I found Shamar when I was in fact on the trail of Olivier Bertevas.

While trying to turn the car around for the umpteenth time in a narrow road on the outskirts of St Pol, I noticed a man looking at me with some interest. I asked him if he could direct me to Rue Chateaubriand, where Olivier lived. He answered in excellent English that he was sorry he could not, except that it was in a certain general direction which he indicated with a wave of his hand. We conversed a little more and I discovered that his name was Jean-Marie Prigent and he had been an onion-seller in Bristol for many years. I told him that I was looking for Oliver Bertevas. Prigent said he knew him well but could not tell me where he lived. 'But his partner, Cueff, lives just down the road from here" he added.

Shamar Cueff's welcome would not have disappointed a long-lost brother. I doubt whether he had really believed that I would turn up in Brittany but he seemed genuinely delighted to see me. We drank large glasses of wine, he gave me two huge lettuces to take back to my wife in Kerlouan and a packet of biscuits for my two year old daughter who had accompanied me in my searches and slept in the back seat of the car for the best part of the day. I noticed he had in a place of some prominence on the side-board a filthy copy of a book I had given him in exchange for half a sack of onions in Cardiff.

I assumed he must have brought it home amongst the empty sacks.

Shamar Cueff's house is in Lagat Vran (the Crow's Eye) a tiny village around a fork in the roads to Roscoff, St Pol de Leon and Morlaix. It's a fairly small detached house in a pleasant spot with a large garden growing rows of artichokes and onions.

I was extremely relieved to discover that Cueff and Bertevas were not in Cardiff. For a variety of reasons I had to postpone my visit to Brittany more than once and it was nearly mid-September by the time I arrived in Roscoff. If the two had made their annual pilgrimage to Wales they would have left Roscoff some weeks earlier.

But now that I had arrived Shamar was overjoyed and full of enthusiasm to assist me in my researches. Here was a friend whom he could easily lead astray in the numerous cafés dotted throughout the small towns and villages. I was ordered to arrive early the next day – in good time for lunch – after which we would commence with the great work.

When I arrived the following day Shamar was busy sowing onion seeds for 1979, tiny black seeds. In a bowl beside him were seeds he had collected in 1977, these were seeds he was now sowing in the ground. In another bowl nearby he had some seeds which he had collected that year (1978). Those were being dried for sowing in the following year. "You can't keep the seeds for more than two years" he explained. By next February the seeds he was then planting would be ready to transplant and they would be fully grown and ready to harvest in July and August.

He had been up early that morning and sold some of his artichokes. As a result he was in the mood for some celebrating. But before we left he introduced me to the taste of raw artichoke. He took a knife, encrusted with dirt from his pocket. It was not unlike the knife, from the point of view of cleanliness, to the knife he used to cut bread and reeds when in Cardiff. He cut a fine artichoke and then showed me how to pluck each leaf in turn and eat the white part at the base of the leaves. Then he used the knife again to cut away the seeds at the top of the vegetable so that the white cone could be eaten. It is hard and comparatively tasteless but excellent for the stomach, said Shamar. "You eat one of these raw every day and you will never get stomach trouble" he insisted. And since Shamar was probably less considerate of his stomach than most of us, I had no cause to argue in the face of such expert advice!

We loaded the car with about a dozen empty wine bottles and drove to St Pol. Our first stop was at a supermarket where the empty bottles were quickly replaced by an equal number of full ones. Then we called at a café for a couple of glasses of wine and a Ricard each, just to be sure that our palates and stomachs would be suitably appreciative of the lunch which Shamar's wife was preparing for us. One of the walls was almost entirely covered by a watercolour picture of St Pol, fields of artichokes, a few houses, typical of the area, in the centre the tower of the celebrated 'Kreisker' and a little to one side, the twin towers of the Cathedral. On the opposite wall was a painting done from the Roscoff coast – a picture of the islands, alive with the movement of the waves; one in which I could almost feel the gentle force of a salty breeze and smell the profusion of flowers. I noticed that the name of the artist was Prigent – a very common name in the area. I had already met one retired onion-seller with that name and I was soon to meet another. The other walls of the café were covered with rows of football teams from some league or other. It included the names of teams from all parts of Brittany, including Rennes and Quiberon but as it was still early in the football season each team had only played three matches.

But if mid-September was early as far as the football season was concerned, these were not early days in the onion-sellers season. In past years Shamar and Olivier would already have been at work in Cardiff and the Valleys, weeks earlier, and two or three Johnnies I was to interview a few days later claimed that the two were back there again this Autumn. The fact that I insisted that I had seen Shamar, talked, drank and had lunch with him did not appear to impress them at all! "I had been saying for years that I was in Cardiff for the last time; I said so again last year, and this time I have kept my word" said Shamar. "Mind, I wouldn't be surprised if Bertevas would be quite happy to go if he had company – but I'm too old now".

74

The famous Kreisker of St. Pol de Leon.

We returned in good time for lunch – chopped onions on slices of tomato for starters followed by slices of pork with broad beans, salad and a very pleasant sauce. The meal was rounded off with pieces of cake. With a couple of glasses of red wine the meal extended luxuriously – it was simple, but prepared beautifully and presented with pride. Shamar often seemed happy enough in the old shop in Bute Street with his potage and apple tart and pints of beer in the Custom House but this was his home – this was where he belonged – here with his gentle wife as neat as her home with her eyes quietly reproachful and disapproving when the old Johnny would say something outrageous. Although, more often than not it was the *way* in which he said things which earned the disapproval.

After lunch we went looking for Olivier, when we arrived at his house we found all the windows wide open but no one answered our knocks. I got the feeling that Shamar was rather pleased – I had already sensed that he did not get on too well with Madame Bertevas and anyway he could lead me to one of the cafés for a quiet afternoon. I soon learnt that Cueff had the reputation, even amongst the hard-drinking fraternity of the onion-sellers, of having a great liking for the bottle. There was also considerable respect for him as a hard worker.

It was about a week later when I actually met Olivier in his home in Brittany. He lives in a small but delightful semi-detached in a quiet street on the outskirts of St Pol de Leon. Behind the house he has a large vegetable garden backing on to open countryside. I joked that he lived in St Pol's 'Rhiwbina'. He smiled and seemed pleased with the description although one was more aware of the proximity of the countryside in this part of St Pol than in Rhiwbina, one of Cardiff's middle-class suburban areas. He also had a number of rabbit hutches in the garden although they were all empty at the time. Occasionally he would breed rabbits to sell to local butchers or for his own pot. The state of his lawn also worried him as a mole was busy pushing up great mounds of earth. We had a long discussion about the best ways of getting rid of moles. I told him about the exceptional talents of two sheep-dogs my father owned, both were first-class mole-catchers. With a slightly sad smile Oliver said it had been high time for him to retire from his trade and end the annual migration to Cardiff. "Mind you, I'm prepared to bet that if I said I'd go Jimmy would have been ready to come with me". I suspected that it would not have taken much persuading to get either to make another trip and I could not decide who was mainly responsible that both were in the warmth of their homes rather than having their limbs frozen stiff on draughty Cardiff street corners. Olivier had not been idle that summer, however, he had been tidying local gardens while his wife spent her mornings looking after one of the grand-children.

It was a strange experience seeing Bertevas in a totally different environment – relaxing among such pleasant surroundings in the warmth of a September summer and the smells of the earth. This was nevertheless the same Olivier that I had talked to so many times in Cardiff, the same shy, yet warm smile, the crooked nose, the same overalls; it could almost have been the same cigarette as clumsily rolled as ever and the light extinguished three-quarters of an inch from his lips, the same feet in the same slippers in the same clogs.

As we went up the stairs to the house – the living area as happens so often in Brittany was above the garage – he kicked off his clogs and shuffled up in his slippers. I gave him a newspaper cutting from the *South Wales Echo* which reported the death of Olivier's brother-in-law and former colleague, Vincent Cabioch. I had received the cutting a few days earlier from another Johnny, Lom an Du from Plouescat who had kept it for many years but had not had the opportunity to pass it on to Bertevas. Olivier showed the picture and the story to his wife, she was Cabioch's sister. She stared at it for a moment before handing it back to Olivier with no flicker of emotion. She went back to feeding the two year child in her care.

As the ferry approaches the new harbour in Roscoff – the deep water part – one gets the impression of a crude, rather rural port. There are very few buildings and hardly any impressions of urban life – quite unlike Plymouth, the town connected to Roscoff by Brittany Ferries. There is just the one place to dock a ship and a high quay, usually crowded with welcoming or waving good-bye to a ship leaving for, and arriving from, Plymouth, Ireland or Spain. There are a lot of large roughly hewen stones around, giving an impression of a job yet to be completed. On the hill between the new port and the old harbour stands the Chapel of Sainte Barbe, in an intoxicating mixture of the scents of pine and salt water. It is a tiny place, with rough stone walls and even cruder steps leading up to its door – crude and rough in spite of a century and a half of pilgrimaging by the wives of the Johnnies. As the ships would sail out of Roscoff the wives would pray for the safe return of their husbands, and the men would acknowledge their prayers and pay homage to Sainte Barbe by lowering the ship's banner.

In those days the onion-sellers sailed from the old harbour which has the town wrapped around it.

They would sail out between Enez Ty Saozon and the chapel and it was to this same harbour that the pilgrims would walk in procession on Sante Barbe's Pardon in July. I recall being shown pictures of that Pardon – one a photograph of worshippers kneeling outside the chapel and the other of the people filing across the beach towards the harbour and the centre of the town. 'Peta Claude' Corre, a very interesting old Johnny, said the pictures must be old as that part of the beach was now filled in to carry the road which skirts the coast. They were in fact dated 1935.

One warm September afternoon in 1978 I sat outside the chapel contemplating something Jean-Marie Cueff had told me. "We always came here before sailing to Cardiff, a few days before going, to put some money in the box. We were making sure that we would return safely". Then I heard a voice by my side. "You are welcome to go inside and to look around the place". To my disappointment I realized the speaker was referring to the Société Langouste buildings down below us. I thanked him and said I would certainly take advantage of the opportunity when I had a little more time. To the east of us a long cargo boat, low in the water, throbbed its way with a load of sand in the direction of Morlaix. Looking in the other direction it was very obvious why it had been necessary to build a new harbour in Roscoff. The tide was far out and there was no hope that the most shallow boat could weave a way out to sea at that hour. But there is still evidence of activity. The lobster pots piled high around the quay point to a thriving local fishing industry. I thought it might be interesting to have a conversation with the man sitting beside me. I could hardly have been more fortunate. From his appearance I had assumed that he was middle-aged, in fact François Gueguen was 76 and was an old onion-seller. He had started selling onions in Scotland with his father in 1913 when he was 11 years of age. As we walked back towards the old harbour he recalled the early days of his trade. "It was from there the near side of that quay, that we would load the onions" he said. "We were at the mercy of the tides and the wind in those days. I remember that the ships were mostly from Treguier and Paimpol. They would sail from here full of onions and return loaded with coal".

He recalled the years of hardship – his father was killed in 1916. After the war he returned to Britain to sell onions with an uncle, this time in Kendall and Middlesborough. "I remember seeing horses being led up from the pits in Durham in 1926 – they were as blind as moles". He went on to talk of his experiences. "I would carry 20 strings of onions – that was more than a 100 pounds – on the stick (ar vaz) on my back. I was just thankful that it would get lighter as the day went on". We walked on, past Mary Stuart's house, until we got to the church Notre Dame Croaz Baz where he showed the two stone cannons embedded in the tower. Their purpose was to try and scare the English who from time to time in the past would plunder the town. Today, there is a much warmer welcome to the British, at least to judge by the luxurious hotels to attract the tourists and amongst the Johnnies one only finds the fondest memories for those parts of "England" which had been their second home for almost an entire lifetime.

I had heard somewhere, or maybe read in Yves-Marie Rudel's novel, *Johnny de Roscoff*, of a café that was an important centre of the Johnnies. I have since learnt that there were many such cafés. One afternoon, in complete ignorance and innocence I asked Shamar Cueff whether he had heard of this café. "C'mon, we'll go there now" he said, grabbing his cap, boots and wiping his lips with the back of his hand. I argued that I wanted to return early to Karlouan that day. "Gast *, we'll be

* A common Breton oath meaning, literally, whore or bitch.

no time at all. You will learn a lot there" said Shamar.

The *Bar des Johnnies* (this café had no connection whatsoever with the places where deals were made, and bargains struck in bygone days) is on the road into Roscoff from St Pol de Leon. If the place was not what I had been expecting it was no less useful and certainly no less entertaining for that. The bar was full of former onion-sellers of all ages, and the red-headed man behind the bar was also an ex-Johnny. We exchanged greetings and talked a little in Breton until everyone had discovered the purpose of my visit.

Then they all switched to English, the accents revealing clearly where each one had been selling his onions. I talked to a fairly youngish man who had been operating from Wrexham until 1974. He talked about some of the villages he used to visit – Rhosllannerchrugog, Ruabon, Coedpoeth and he tried out a few phrases of Welsh too! Another fairly young man who had been an onion-seller in Poole, Dorset was François Danielou. He had left the old trade and now worked for Brittany Ferries. "They were OK, the people of Poole" he said, "but they were a little..." and he placed his index finger under his nose and tilted his head back a little. Suddenly, he looked at his watch, drained his third glass of wine in a single gulp, jumped on his bike and pedalled madly towards the ferry-port. His ship was about to sail.

I settled comfortably into the conversation and the wine. The bar was typical of thousands in Brittany and France. There was a juke-box with a good choice of Presley records, the bar and the tables were formica topped and there were plenty of plastic stools. Alan Castell was holding court. Alan spent his lifetime in the Liverpool area so I was interested to learn that he had a good knowledge of Welsh. "I sold onions regularly to the Professor of Welsh at Liverpool University" he said. "I can't remember his name but I remember that he lived in Crosby". I assumed that he was referring to Professor J. Glyn Davies. When I talked to him Alan Castell was very lame and leaned heavily on his two walking sticks – "My two horse power" – even to walk to the bar. With their help he could just about shuffle into the *Bar des Johnnies* where he spent most of his time in the company of his friends. He talked about Henri Olivier from Santec, the first Johnny Onions who had sailed with three neighbours and a load of onions to Plymouth in 1828. "Santec came under the administration of Roscoff in those days" he explained. "Santec and Roscoff were separated administratively in 1920".

He talked about selling onions in Formby when war was declared in 1939. "I had to sell my onions at a big loss and return to France immediately – I lost the bloody lot". He took a franc piece from his pocket.

"That's all I had on me when I got home". Alan used to take his family with him to England every year. "We used to return to the same house in Formby – my daughter went to school in Liverpool". During the spring and summer when he was not selling onions Alan, with the help of another onion-seller, would collect loads of seaweed from the beaches to sell to the farmers. Seaweed is the manure mostly used to enrich the fields in the countryside of the red onion. The man who helped Alan to collect and sell the seaweed was also in the bar, a man of 77 who had sold onions in London throughout his working life. Unlike Alan, he was as lively on his feet as many a person half his age.

The two talked about the years immediately after the war – years of genuine hardship. "We would be doing more than one job" said Castell. "I remember working all night loading ships. Then a few hours of sleep before going out to work in the fields. As well as that, we would help to repair the harbour after the damage of the war".

I bought a bottle of wine, made my excuses and left. One of the younger ex-Johnnies said an original farewell in what was probably the only Welsh words he knew. "Cig moch a bara menyn" (bacon and bread and butter). "We'll be no time at all', I growled at Cueff after realising that we had been in the café for almost two hours. "Hell, you had plenty of fun and some good stuff, didn't you?" was the reply. Since there was more than a grain of truth in what he said I did not argue.

Jean-Marie Roignant – or Shamar Roignant – made quite an impression on me, even before I saw his face. I had called on Shamar Cueff and as Madam Cueff was ushering me towards the kitchen I heard someone shouting gleefully in Welsh, "Dos adra, diawl bach, tyd ma tro nesa!'' (Get lost, you little devil, come next time). And he said it in the gloriously broad accent of Caernarfon. But by now Roignant can remember very little Welsh; in fact he spent very few years in Wales. He started selling onions in 1924 when he was 12 years of age, mostly on the Isle of Anglesey.

He obviously had a soft spot for the island. ''I was no higher than ''three apples'' – *comme trois pommes* – when I was selling onions in Llangefni market'', he recalled. On that first visit to Wales he earned a total of 200 francs, about 35 shillings, and his food. He was one of 24 Johnnies based in Caernarfon. ''I learnt to speak Welsh while playing with the children in the town'' he said ''but then I went to sell in Scotland where I worked until I retired. So I have forgotten a lot of my Welsh''.

He used to come over from Roscoff to Caernarfon in a sailing ship, helping to unload the cargo of onions on arrival. Those onions would then be sold across the length and breadth of North Wales – as far as the village Nefyn on the tip of the Llyn peninsula and across to Llandudno on the North coast. His fellow workers would also take lorry loads of onions to Chester and Bala – they had a 'botteleur', a man stringing onions for them in Chester – and from those centres they would be selling in and around the towns and villages of Corwen, Ruthin, Oswestry and Betws-y-Coed. The company to which Roignant belonged owned two 13 horse-power Ford vans. ''They had only two gears, no battery and wooden wheels but they could carry a ton of onions. I used to drive them myself in 1925 when I was just 13 – not on long journeys, just in the countryside around Caernarfon. The children I would play with couldn't believe their eyes''. I could easily believe that. Roignant is a small man, stocky, quick in thought and deed. He took snuff. He reeled a long list of villages around Caernarfon. ''I would go to Bethesda every other Saturday, to Portdinorwic once every three weeks and I remember going to Rhosneigr and the place with the very long name, Llanfair PG''. He said that he remembered the Dolgarrog disaster. ''I'm sure we left the place minutes before the dam broke. We were on our way home from Corwen fair and had stopped in the hotel in Dolgarrog. We didn't know anything about the disaster until a couple of days later when we saw pictures of dead sheep and cattle in the paper".

He recalled believing that the farmers in Anglesey must have been quite rich. "Everyone of them seemed to have had an Austin 7, even in those days.

"There were hardly any tractors in the countryside but these little cars were everywhere. The farmers in Anglesey must have been rich". I noticed that Roignant had two tractors, the little Fergusons. He said that he used to have a small-holding at one time but that he had stopped farming when he got to retirement age.

"Another thing that amazed me in Wales was the skill of the sheep-dogs. I remember being surprised at the number of sheep, too, but the dogs – they were cleverer than me. I was in Ruthin market one day when a herd of sheep bolted through the town. In a flash a dog went after them and in no time at all he had rounded them up and brought them back to where they were supposed to be. I bought one of those sheep-dogs and brought it back to Brittany with me – God, that was a clever dog. My greatest pleasure when I was in Caernarfon would be to watch a dog at work with a herd of sheep or cattle. I once spent half a day in a sheep-dog trail in Cerrig-y-drudion. I simply couldn't understand how a dog could guide three sheep in that way".

He talked about his life as a Johnny Onions in Caernarfon. "We lived on soup and bacon. We would have a large bacon joint; the man who did the cooking would cut it into slices, he would then put the meat behind his back and pick a piece for each one without looking at the plate. Sometimes he would cheat a bit, so that someone who could not eat fatty meat would get the fattiest piece of the lot. We would spend all our time playing dominoes. We had to go to church, of course, we used to attend the Roman Catholic church which is about a mile from Caernarfon castle. The "boss", Louis Roignant, used to give us two pence each for the collection plate".

As the surname suggests the two were related, Louis was Shamar's uncle. But in spite of being related, the two never got on. "We would quarrel like a cat and dog all the time". In 1927 Shamar joined another company which sold onions on

83

Guernsey. "I remember there were a lot of grapes and tomatoes on the island. I went back there two years ago and nothing had changed. Life was just as slow and relaxed".

Then in 1929 Roignant set his sights on more northern lands, Scotland. He first went to Dundee before settling eventually for Perth. It was evident that the places which kindled his deepest love were the glens and the countryside. He talked a great deal of his frequent visits to Oban, Balachulish, Glencoe and Fort William. His wife and daughter spent two seasons with him in Perth, in fact his daughter was only three years old when she came on her first visit to Scotland. "But in no time she could speak English better than any of us" said Roignant. But his pretty, black-haired wife hardly learnt any English at all during her stays in Scotland. "But she learnt to string onions as well as any of us. She could string half a ton of onions in a day". In Perth he was the "boss" and he had eight in his company, including his wife, his daughter, an uncle (not Louis!) and other hired workers.

He had a brother who used to sell onions from Stornaway on the Isle of Lewis. In fact, according to Shamar, his brother was on the island the night before Commander Charcot sailed on his tragic journey on the *Pourquoi Pas*. He and his entire crew were lost in the North Sea. "My brother must have been the last Frenchman, apart from the crew, to have seen Charcot alive. He had been invited to a party by some of the sailors that night before they sailed" said Roignant. He showed me a letter, post-marked Stornaway, which he had received from his brother. His brother was killed in the Second World War.

Roignant spoke very good English with a strong Scottish accent. He then talked about his favourite writers, Zola and Solzhenitsyn. Cueff showed him a copy of a Welsh book I had once written on Brittany. As he turned the pages he noticed a poem in Breton by Roman Huon, which he read with obvious delight. "Hell, it's good, very political, excellent" he said. It was enough to set him off on another track. He began criticizing the treatment Roscoff had been getting from the Government. "Twenty years ago, this was the richest little town in Brittany – perhaps in the whole of France. The soil is excellent and it's possible to get three crops a year from it – early potatoes, cauliflowers and onions". It was obvious that he had a point when one considers the acres under heavy crops of artichokes and cauliflowers.

*   *   *

"Do you know where the highest railway station in Britain can be found?" asked the little onion-seller. "No" I replied, and even if I did know my answer would still have been the same. It would have been shameful to have spoiled his story. Like many another onion Johnny this one delighted in his knowledge of the area which had been his second home. "Blaenavon" he replied with absolute certainty. This man's name was Jean-Marie Prigent, from the tiny village of Lagat Vran. With his neighbour Cueff he had been selling his onions in North Gwent for many years. Cueff and I returning from a visit to St Pol where he had been replenishing his dwindling stock of wine when he saw his former colleague. "Come over to the café" shouted my companion "this chap wants a word with you". And thus we arrived at the *Rendez-vous des Amis* where I learnt all about the railway station in Blaenavon.

There was no need to question this man, he just blurted out his story. He had been selling onions in Blaenavon since he was 12 and the first lesson he had learnt was not to leave his onions in front of the house while going round to knock on the back door. "The sheep would be there in a flash and they would nibble a piece off every onion in sight – they never ate a whole one" he said. "I remember seeing sheep taking whole loaves out of women's shopping baskets in Broad Street.

"Life was hard in those days. I can feel that *vaz* on my shoulder to this day. Sometimes the stick with its heavy load would rub my shoulder until it bled and by the time I get back that evening my shirt would be stuck in the dried blood. Mind you, life was hard in Wales those days too, bloody hard. Do you know where Pwll-du is? It's three miles over the mountain from Blaenavon. All you'll find there is a pub, a farm and a row of houses. In 1923 I remember that everyone in Pwll-du worked in a limestone quarry, digging lime to build the Blaenavon steel-works with the horses pulling the loads out. When I went there I would sell a string of onions in every house – nobody ever refused".

85

After 45 seasons it was not surprising to hear Prigent describing Blaenavon in such detail and with such obvious delight. "I would start at the bottom of Broad Street, sell a few strings in the butcher's shop, and then the pubs – I also did a good trade in the pubs". He listed his journeys in more recent years when he and a companion using a van would sell the onions and back in the warehouse they had a stringer or 'botteleur', working full time. The names slipped sweetly off his tongue. On Monday both would be selling in Abersychan and Talywaun; Tuesday in Abertillery; Wednesday in Talybont on Usk and Brecon; Thursday in Aberfan, Treharris, Trelewis, Bedlinog, Fochriw and Rhymni; on Friday, one would be selling in Tredegar and the other in Blaenavon; on Saturday, both of them and the stringer would be selling in Tredegar. The week after would be as follows: Monday, Dowlais and Merthyr; Tuesday, Abertillery; Wednesday, one in Ebbw Vale and the other in Aberbeeg; Thursday, Aberdare, Rhigos, Glynneath and Hirwaun; Friday, one in Blaenavon and the other in Brynmawr; Saturday, one in Blackwood and the other in Brynmawr. They would also be making occasional visits to Gilwern, Llangynidr, Llanfoist and Abergavenny.

"But we never forced anyone to buy. We knew where to sell and who was likely to buy" he said. The old nickname of "bell-breaker" given to the early Johnnies was certainly no fair description of him.

Prigent changed his tone and turned to Shamar Cueff. "You, too, are now suffering because you spent so much time away from home – your pension is less than it could have been". Prigent explained that while he was selling onions in Britain he could not contribute towards his pension. He could only contribute while working at home in Brittany – driving a lorry for a local company. Sometimes employers would try to help their workers to get around this difficulty, but Prigent had no such luck.

*　　　　　*　　　　　*

Lom an Du, Lom an Dukik, Guillaume Le Duff, William Le Duff – all forms of the same name, with the same person concealing behind this variety of names. While seeking

86

background information on the Johnnies I had contacted a number of newspapers and magazines in Brittany asking for assistance from any reader who might be able to help. Among the letters and packages which I received during the following weeks and months was one from a missionary in Sri Lanka, the Rev. Father Albert Pleiber. In his letter, Father Pleiber directed me to the hamlet of Pen ar Prad, some three kilometres from Plouescat. There, said the letter, lives a retired onion seller, with a good story to tell. If the Reverend Father could take the trouble to write from Sri Lanka the least I could do was to follow his suggestion.

Not many onion-sellers live in the vicinity of Plouescat; it is a village on the periphery of their district. The first time I went looking for him, I stopped by a little cross in the village and asked a well-groomed woman whether she could tell me where Lom an Dukik lived. She smiled and said "Ah, you use the Breton form of his name". She pointed to a small cottage, but said that he was not at home, otherwise the door would be open. "He must be out in the fields harvesting artichokes" adding that he had a number of fields, some of which were a few miles away. I decided to call on the following day, but before leaving I looked around the village and at Lom's cottage – a pretty, rustique place that might have looked good on a picture post card. It was a simple place, rather improverished, onion seeds were drying in the sun in front of the door with an aggressive dog keeping guard.

When I returned on the following day, Lom an Du was at home, having just finished his mid-day meal. He had obviously heard that I had been looking for him on the previous day and he appeared strangely suspicious. "You're not a Welshman" he said. It was a statement of fact, not a question. "You were in the village yesterday and you were speaking Breton". I replied that I could speak some Breton, but I was most certainly Welsh and I explained how I had heard of him – from Sri Lanka. "Aaah!, Pleiber", he answered, relaxing, "you'll have to come with me to meet his family". He explained that his wife was ill in bed but since he had been selling artichokes that morning he looked forward to a quiet afternoon. He offered me lunch but I excused myself saying that I had eaten before arriving. For some strange reason he assumed I was a teetotaller and poured me a glass of lemonade while helping himself to a generous glass of red wine. We then talked about his experiences as an onion-seller.

He had first come over to Wales in the early twenties when he was fifteen years of age. His mother had died and he was one of three children. "Too many Johnnies were coming over in those days. A total of 15,000 came over between the wars" he said. "We had very little education although I was a little more fortunate than most. I had gone to school when I was nine, but those who had gone to sell onions in England when they were nine had no chance to get some education". Lom's mother had died when he was eleven and his father had then announced that there would be no more school for him. Nevertheless, he had managed to get some occasional schooling during the following two years. "When I went selling onions in Cardiff I used to buy newspapers and try to read them after the day's work. You must remember that in those days I spoke very little French; I had been taught through the medium of French in school and I could read and write the language fairly well but I wasn't really at home speaking the language until I went to the army in 1930. I spent most of my years in the army in Algeria. When I returned to sell onions in Cardiff after being in the army I remember going back to see a lady, she was French, who had been one of my old customers. She praised my French and said it had improved a lot while I had been in the army. I never speak anything but Breton to my wife and my two sons are also fluent in the language".

He talked of his early days in Cardiff. "In those days the ship would come up the West Dock as far as the old Spillers mill. There we would unload the onions ourselves; if the dockers did the work we'd have to pay them and that meant less profit. Then we'd go to the Butetown Tavern for a pint. Of course, we sold a lot of onions in pubs and someone would always buy us a half before we left. At first, I worked in a company of 20 sellers in Cardiff, then I went on my own. I would work like hell, every day, Sunday too. In the end it was all too much to me. And my wife was not in very good health and she worried a lot when I went away. I bought some more land and tried to make a better life for myself without going to Britain. I thought of going over three years ago with Olivier Bertevas but in the end I stayed at home.

"I liked going though and I made many good friends. I still write to some people in Cardiff and Penarth – they were very good to me. All except the police. I don't have happy memories of them. They once suspected me of murder and on another time they came to ask me questions in connection with a robbery. It's not a nice thing to happen to anyone, especially in a foreign country. Someone found the body of a murdered woman in a field near Penylan, Cardiff, near the route I used to travel daily. The police came to ask about my whereabouts on that day. One policeman kept coming back and I became very frightened – my hair turned completely white and it remained like that until I returned to Brittany. I remember that policeman asking me whether I had blood on my clothes. I became so worried, I remember one day that I was crying while selling onions in Cardiff. On another occasion there had been a robbery in Whitchurch and the police came again to interview me and ask where I had been at four o'clock the day before".

But apart from those bitter experiences, Lom had reasonably happy memories of those years he spent in Cardiff. "A coloured man once snatched a string of onions from my hand. I ran after him and he dropped the onions. On another occasion a man came up to me in a pub and said "Your're a stranger here; we don't want your sort here". Then two men who were sitting nearby said to him "Your're the stranger here, get out of here and leave him alone". I had plenty of friends in Cardiff".

He got up and took a box from a cupboard. It contained letters from former clients in Cardiff and a newspaper cutting from the *South Wales Echo*, January 16, 1973 reporting on the death of a former friend and colleague. "Vincent Cabioch died last week when boarding a ship at Roscoff, when he slipped on the gang plank and fell on to the rocks between the vessel and the quay". The story went on to mention Cabioch's popularity – he had spent 35 seasons in Cardiff. "If you see Olivier Bertevas during the next few days I would like you to give him this cutting. Vincent was Olivier's brother-in-law" said Lom. I promised to do so, and indeed, saw Bertevas a few days later and gave him the cutting.

I asked him about the problem of contributing towards a pension. "As I was completely self-employed in the latter years things weren't too bad. Since I am a farmer with my own farm nobody needed to know where I was – whether I was at home farming in Pen ar Prad or selling onions in England. So I was able to make a full contribution towards my pension".

He pointed to the *lit clos*, the traditional Breton bed which looks like a cupboard and can be closed like one. "That's where I was born, and my father before me". His unmarried son, a solicitor in Morlaix, still living with his parents, slept in it now, said Lom.

Lom surprised me with his knowledge of Welsh. He did not know enough Welsh for us to converse in the language, but certainly knew enough to sell onions or to ask the way. This was surprising since Caridff had always been his base and even when he was a member of a 'company' of sellers who would go out of Cardiff he always went towards the English-speaking areas of South-East Wales and even into England. "Before the war I remember going in a van to Hereford, Abergavenny and even as far as Symmonds Yat to sell onions. Even so, I realized that the two languages had a lot in common even though I did not often come into contact with Welsh". Lom an Dukik was a remarkable person in this respect. He had also kept in touch with a few people in Cardiff even though it was quite a few years since his last visit to this country.

When the war broke out in 1939 he had returned immediately to Brittany and he spent part of the war working as a translator on the Italian front, near Turin. We broke off our conversation and walked across the sandy farmyard to the farm which was the home of Father Pleiber's family.

We had a warm welcome and were shown around one of the largest farmhouses in the Plouescat area. Afterwards I promised to call again in a few days time to get some strings of onions to take back to some of his former customers in Cardiff. I called twice but on both occasions he was not at home and I had to return empty-handed.

*   *   *

I have heard it said that dogs often look like their owners – or vice-versa! It is certainly true that Johnny Onions looked like his customers. Naturally their accents, when they spoke English (or in some instances Welsh) made it easy to identify where they had been selling their onions. But they also appeared to have assimilated something of the behaviour, or the bearing of their former customers – as if some part of the land to which they migrated had become a part of their whole being. Jean-Marie Prigent, who spent almost 20 seasons selling onions in Bristol, was a good example. He is a cousin of the Jean-Marie Prigent who used to work from Blaenavon but their names was about all that was similar in the two. The Blaenavon Prigent was a lively character, a rapid conversationalist ready with a torrent of information – a true valleys man. His cousin, the Bristol Prigent was a calmer personality whose accent and conduct was reminiscent of a respectable middle-class inhabitant of that city.

He arrived in Bristol for the first time in 1920 at the age of eleven. Within three days he was out selling onions on his own. "For the first two days I went out with my father" he said "and after that I was on my own, On the third day he put a piece of paper with the address of the store on it – in case I got lost – and sent me on my way. I was the eldest of seven children, so as soon as I was old enough to do some work it was off to England". A few years later his father changed his patch and went to Glasgow to sell onions but Jean-Marie Prigent continued in Bristol, except for three seasons he spent in Cardiff. "I didn't like the beer in Cardiff, and the pubs were shut on Sundays".

Sunday opening or no Sunday opening, when Prigent and his fellow onion-sellers were in Bristol Sunday morning was a time for worship. "We used to attend St. Mary's Roman Catholic Church on the quay. The boss would give us each 2 pence for the collection – but we would only put *one* on the plate and spend the other on an ice-cream cornet or a packet of fags".

Although Prigent worked in Cardiff for only three seasons, his connection with the city was closer. At one time, the onions were transported by sea from Roscoff to Cardiff and then from Cardiff to Bristol by rail. "In the years between the wars a

Jean-Marie Prigent — a man of Bristol.

shipload of onions would arrive in Cardiff every three weeks and I would go there to meet the ship, help unload it and get the onions transported to our base. My mother made the arrangements in Brittany, bought the onions and sent the loads over. At times we would be away from home for four to six months at a time. It was quite difficult to anticipate when the next ship would be arriving in Cardiff. I was at sea for a week on one occasion, there was no wind to swell the sails. My father was once on a sailing ship which took a month to get to Glasgow – and he suffered terribly from sea-sickness. But, usually, 24 hours was long enough, provided there was a fair wind, for those little ships to make the crossing'', said Prigent. His father had ended his seasonal migrations to Britain in 1935 but he had lived until 1977 when he died at the age of 96. Jean-Marie had three brothers who also carried on the family tradition up to 1939.

In those days Jean-Marie Prigent was used to very long journeys. He used to go selling around Bath, Trowbridge and Weston-Super-Mare, as well as Bristol and the surrounding villages. ''I would start at half past five in the morning and push my bike, laden with a mountain of onions, all the way to Weston – 22 miles it was. And I had to sell every string before starting back. The boss would always be telling us ''Don't bring one onion back here, we've got plenty in the store''. Years later we would take a lorry and easily travel fifty or sixty miles a day to sell our onions''.

When war broke out, it proved a difficult and hectic time for the onion men. ''I was in Bristol at the time and we had seven or eight tons of onions to sell. We could only drop the price and we had to sell the lot to a local merchant before returning on a ship from Southampton to Cherbourg. Mind you, some of the Johnnies stayed in England and joined the armed forces there. I know one man from Roscoff who did not return after the war was decared and his family heard nothing of him until he walked in the house five years later having been in India and all sorts of places. He could not write home to tell his family where he was. I was not accepted for military service because of an accident I had when I was 20''.

He described how he had been working in and around

Roscoff during the war years, mostly on farms and he remembered with pleasure the day when the Americans liberated that part of Brittany. "I was working in a field when I saw them coming. I asked if anyone had cigarettes and someone threw a packet at me. Another one asked whether I liked chocolate and before I said a word I had a large piece in my a hand. I asked if anyone could sell me a pair of boots. A black American sat down beside me, he took his boots off and offered them to me. "Are they OK?" he asked me. "They're fine" I replied, "How much do you want for them?". "Five hundred francs?" he suggested. I paid him gladly – I had worn nothing but my clogs since the beginning of the war. Clogs are fine in the winter in the cold and wet, but they are much too hot to wear in summer".

Prigent returned to Bristol after the war but his annual visits did not last for long. He went over for the last time in 1951. After the war he would take his load of onions by boat to Portsmouth and from there to Bristol by lorry. "We would use a primus stove to cook. But they were difficult days because of the food rationing – there was not much meat. Of course, we had our ration books like everyone else". He said that he once got into difficulty because he was taking a number of packets of tea back to Brittany. As he and his fellow workers rarely drank tea they were taking their tea ration home to their wives. But the customs men would not believe their story – they were convinced the Johnnies had been buying tea on the black market.

After retiring from onion selling Prigent worked as an agent for a local merchant buying vegetables from farmers in the Roscoff and St Pol de Leon area. "The children don't want to follow in the old trade – I have a daughter who is a teacher in Brest and a son in Paris. The young people want to go to Paris – they don't want to stay on the farms around here. They get better money by going away". We ended our conversation with Prigent asking me about the price of beer and cigarettes in Britain today. He appeared amazed at the march of inflation. "I remember paying – I don't remember the year – six pence for a pint of beer, two pence for the Woodbines and a shilling for twenty Players. God, how things change". He added that his

94

favourite beer was George's of Bristol – a brew I had to admit to being ignorant.

"Glesca's ma toon"

I first met 'Peta Claude' Corre sitting on a little wall on the old quay in Roscoff, staring out to sea. This was his favourite spot where he would sit from two o'clock onwards every afternoon. I was walking along the waterfront with François Guegen, who was pushing his bike, the type with an engine above the front wheel. The little engine has a wheel which turns against the bicycle's tyre – a simple principle but reasonably effective as these bikes are capable of travelling quite rapidly.

When Guegen saw his friend we walked over and he introduced me to Peta Claude. "Come for a chat, I've got plenty of stuff for you in the house" said Peta Claude immediately and started shuffling painfully towards his first floor flat in Rue Jules Ferry. He leant very heavily on his walking stick but if his movement was desperately slow his speech was rapid and a strong Glasgow accent coloured his English. On the door of his apartment his name, Claude Corre, was embroidered over a piece of Scottish tartan. But even though his name is Claude Corre to the people of Glasgow he was 'Peta Claude' – indeed many people in Roscoff called him by that name. He invited me to sit at the table and took a box out of a cupboard. He handed me a cutting from a Scottish newspaper. The cutting contained a picture of him with a splendid string of onions around his neck and behind him on the wall was a picture of Robbie Burns.

I noted a few lines of the story: "The strangest most warm-hearted tribute to Robbie Burns comes from a stocky little 'Ingan Johnnie' who believes with all his heart in the 'Auld Alliance'. He boasts that he has sold onions to four generations of one family in Cellardyke in Fyfe. ('After France, Scotland is ma country and Glesca's ma toon')".

The story went on to explain the circumstances in which the picture was taken. Peta Claude was a guest of honour at a meeting of 'Our's Club' and it was reported that he had sung his own Breton translation of *Ye Banks and Braes*. He showed another picture of himself, a picture taken on his first visit to

"Peta Claude" Corre as an old man shuffling painfully around Roscoff but chatting with great liveliness about his memories.

Scotland in 1920 when he was only eleven years of age. With him in the picture was his father and a tall, successful looking customer. It was a rather amusing picture – a tiny Peta Claude with a large cap on his head, the tall customer and Peta Claude's father, a small man also with a large cap and a heavy moustache. He tipped the contents of the box on the table and I noticed from another newspaper cutting that he claimed Mary Stuart to have been one of his heroines. After all, did she not sail from Tantallon Castle, Berwickshire to Roscoff when she was a mere five years of age in 1548? He then drew my attention to a copy of the letter included amongst the papers, a letter sent by the Roscoff Johnnies to Lady Clementine Churchill at the time of the death of her husband, Winston Churchill.

> "Dear Lady Churchill,
>
> In the name and on behalf of all the Roscoff onion merchants I wish to express to you the deep sorrow and grief we feel on the passing of Sir Winston Churchill. We owe him our gratitude for all he has done for France in the last war and we cannot forget that it is thanks to him that we are free people today and that we are able to come over to your country to bring you our products.
>
> Please accept from us all the sincerest expression of sympathy and may God give you all the strength and courage to bear your great sorrow.
>
> Johnnies de Roscoff".

I never met an onion Johnny with as much enthusiasm for the area where he had been selling as Peta Claude. He was an admirer of Robbie Burns and a staunch follower of Celtic Football Club and he claimed to have never missed a home match. "I was in Hampden Park, I think it was in 1948 when Scotland played Hungary and Puskas was in Hungary's team. What a player – he scored a goal that day. I'm sure the goalkeeper never saw the ball. I was shouting like hell for Scotland but that Puskas was a genius. Aye, I'm a Scotsman, or at least I was a Scotsman when I was in Glasgow. Mind you, some Scots are better than others. Take the people of Greenock, they'd take the sugar from your tea".

We turned to the subject of drink, always a favourite topic of the Johnnies. "I never sold onions on the morning after a Burns Night – I always had a bad head. Usually I would drink

Younger's Strong Ale and whisky on special occasions, like on Burns Night and Hogmanay. I loved a drop of Johnny Walker but I couldn't stand the smell which came from their distillery. Once, I tried to sell onions outside their gates – I had to go away, the smell was terrible. There should have been a law against it". He placed two glasses on the table and filled them with red wine. "First today" he said, raising his glass, "that's what they used to say in Scotland, "First today, never the last, always the first! Iec'hed mad". We drank to Celtic co-operation and understanding.

He talked about his final visit to Scotland then asked me where I was staying in Brittany. I replied that I was staying in Kerlouan. "Ah, Kerlouan" he said. "That's the place for garlic, the best garlic in the world is grown in Kerlouan". Peta Claude was seldom short on exaggeration. "I used to sell three tons of garlic every year between the Glen Eagles and the Central Hotel in Glasgow. Both hotels had French chefs and there was always a welcome for me in either place, and breakfast if I wanted it. I used to sell a lot of onions to those hotels, too. I remember that I would sell four bags (56 lbs each) every week to the Central Hotel, Glasgow, on top of what I would sell to the Glen Eagles and the Grand Hotel, St Andrews".

When he was eleven years old, Peta Claude tried to get some extra work so that he could pay to go to night school. "I managed to get two months of night school for three years, that's all the school I ever had. But I learnt the important things – how to count money, write a bit and read. But I spent far more time learning from experience". When he was about fifteen Peta Claude had a slight brain haemorrhage and had to go to hospital for treatment. After being released he had to go back to the hospital for a weekly check-up from the doctor who had treated him. "I remember the doctor telling my father during one of those check-ups that a lad of my age and state of health should not be living in such conditions. But in no time at all I was out selling onions again, but not too near the hospital just in case one of the doctors should see me".

His opinions of customers were also interesting. "The Italians were good buyers and the French chefs, although the red onion of Roscoff is not their favourite – they prefer the yellow onions

"Peta Claude" Corre as a guest of honour at a Burns' night celebrations.

99

grown around St Brieuc, Langueux and Yffiniac. But those yellow onions, they don't keep so well, you see. I remember the Gorbals in Glasgow full of Jews – they were hard bargainers; but I could do business with them. But the Pakistanis who are there now – I never had much luck with them – always on the lookout for the cheapest stuff''.

The war interrupted his trade like all the other onion-sellers but he was back in 1947. ''We were selling wholesale that first year, the English Government wouldn't let us sell in our traditional way. We took 55 tons to Southampton. After that we were allowed to sell again in our old style, thanks to François Mazeas. He was a very clever man, and determined. It was a long and hard fight before everything was settled but in the end we were given assurances that we could continue our old trade''.

Many of the onion Johnnies I met were enjoying a very comfortable retirement, after a lifetime of considerable hardship. But Peta Claude was living out his last years in surroundings far more drab than most of the others.

His home was a tiny, impoverished flat on the first floor of a very uninspiring building. As I was going out through the front door I noticed a card asking everyone to keep it closed. ''It's bloody cold here in winter'' said Peta Claude. I called to see him many times after that first visit and the last time I saw him he was worrying that he would have to see the doctor soon and probably spend another period in hospital.

We walked together towards his favourite seat on the low wall on the quay, walking very slowly as Peta Claude shuffled painfully along. When we had settled there a smartly dressed French woman came over to us and started nagging the little onion man about his smoking. It was evidently something of a daily discussion as Peta Claude like so many other onion sellers was never without his crude hand-rolled cigarette, nicotine and saliva stained, in the corner of his mouth. He laughed ''Hell, it's my life and my health and I'll do as I like with it''. He spoke without any bitterness and there was no hint of a suggestion that the woman should mind her own business. Before long, the discussion was not about Peta Claude's excessive smoking but about the charm of Robbie Burns's poetry with the little

100

"Peta Claude", on his first visit to Scotland in 1920 when he was 11 years old. His father is on the left and a customer in the centre.

Johnny giving an enthusiastic lecture. This was evidently a Peta Claude she had never seen before and if the two still meet on the quay at Roscoff, I suspect that their conversation is about something of greater consequence than Peta Claude's smoking. After she left us the little onion-seller smiled and said to me "She is really very kind and she worries about me".

*   *   *

Jean Berthou when I met him was an old man. He was born in 1897 and when I met him he had just celebrated his eighty first birthday, but I could hadly have imagined a livelier octogenarian. When I arrived at his house in Crea'h Avel, on the outskirts of Cleder, mid-morning he was busy in his large vegetable garden. At the end of the garden farthest from the house workmen were busy renovating a small cottage. With pride, Jean Berthou, pointed to the massive thickness of the walls, made of huge, crude stones which had somehow been fitted together with incredible neatness. He told me that he did all the gardening himself except for a little help from his nephew who would bring a horse and plough to turn the soil over at the beginning of Spring.

But of greater interest than his activities was a story he told of an experience he had early in his career as an onion-seller. Berthou started selling onions in 1912 when he was fifteen years old. Two years later he was on his way to Scotland when the 1914 war was declared. The war started at the beginning of August and a number of Johnnies had set sail in boats loaded with onions for Britain at the end of June and early July. Those Johnnies had sold a lot of their onions and their warehouses were comparatively empty, but later arrivals were in great difficulties and they were forced to sell their onions at a considerable loss to whoever would buy them. But some others had even greater problems and Jean Berthou was among them. He sailed to Aberdeen on *Les Jumelles*, a sailing ship carrying onions and onion-sellers. While they were at sea war was declared, but in those days there was no means of contacting a sailing ship at sea and *Les Jumelles* accompanied by two other sailing ships, *La Roscovite* and *L'Hermann*, also carrying similar loads continued on their route to Aberdeen.

The first that Jean Berthou and his colleagues heard of the war was when the French consul met them on the quay ordering every one within the enlisting age to return home immediately. After a lot of argument the Bretons were given three days to dispose of the onions. But everyone did not have to leave at the end of three days and those who were either too young or too old to go into the French armed forces were allowed to stay a little longer to sell the remainder of the onions. Jean Berthou was among those who were too young to fight. With the swift departure of so many of the onion-sellers – they went by rail to London before making the short crossing across the channel – another problem arose. The captains would use the onion-sellers to help sail the ships. Now that so many of the onion-sellers had gone home the captains had no crews to sail their ships. Captain Koadou of *La Roscovite* was in the worst predicament of all; besides himself he had one cabin boy, one seaman and an officer to sail his ship home to Roscoff. Koadou was determined not to be blockaded in Aberdeen for the duration of the war so he went looking for volunteers from among the remaining Johnnies to help him to return to Roscoff. He eventually found four prepared to go with him; François Danielou, aged 15 from Roscoff; Jean-Françoise Corre, aged 16 from Roscoff, Claude Creignou, a 65 year old stringer also of Roscoff who was known as 'Glaoda ar sarjant' since he had been a sergeant in the army in 1870 and Jean Berthou aged 17 from Cleder. The ship was loaded with coal in Kircaldy before they set out on their hazardous journey home. It took them nearly a month – not because of the volunteer crew's lack of experience, but because there was no wind. "We were even trying to go looking for wind, but had no luck" said Berthou. It has been said that the captain was also trying to avoid being seen by German warships. But Berthou did not believe that story. He insisted that the only difficulty had been the unusual calm. When *La Roscovite* sailed into Roscoff one morning at the beginning of September 1914 one can only wonder which was the greater, the relief of those on board or the unexpected pleasure of their families and friends.

In a matter of months he was old enough to become a soldier and he fought through to the end of the war. In 1924 he

Jean Berthou, Cleder, picking onion seeds. He was one of the tiny crew that sailed ''La Roscovite'' back from Scotland after World War 1 broke out.

returned to Scotland to renew his former trade. He showed me a picture of himself selling onions with the *vaz* over his shoulder, it had been taken about 1933. But the bicycle was already a more popular and effective tool for carrying strings of onions. "O yes, I had my regular customers. They would never buy onions from another Johnny" he said. He talked about his route – Berwick-on-Tweed, Dunbar, Peebles, Galashiels, Selkirk, Melrose, Kelso – "a lovely country". On his bicycle he would visit each one of those towns once every three weeks. Normally he would be back in Brittany before Christmas. He talked about the route home at the end of the season. "We would usually go by train to Folkestone, sail from there to Boulogne and home by train through Paris. It was a very quick route. Sometimes we would sail from Southampton to Cherbourg and on one or two occasions I remember sailing directly to Morlaix". Like so many other 'ingan Johnnies' I met he had a soft spot in his heart for Scotland. "Now, take Berwick. That was a place to sell onions. All the hotels had French chefs – it was a great place to do business". Although he had retired from selling onions many years ago he had returned to Scotland for a holiday as recently as 1976 – indeed he was obviously very fond of returning to Britain for his holidays although he usually went to Cornwall. It is very convenient crossing from Roscoff to Plymouth.

He was genuinely sad when I said it was time for me to depart and insisted on getting his whisky bottle out as a gesture of solidarity with the land of the hard stuff. He succeeded in detaining me a little longer. He noticed my interest in the antique furniture which graced his living room and insisted that I should have a proper look at everything. In the kitchen was a large table with a bench which went completely around it. It was easy to imagine little children climbing over the bench and with shiny bottoms sliding around to the far side of the table. Hanging from the ceiling was a round wooden disk with eight holes through which eight knives and eight forks could be suspended – or to be more accurate eight forks and eight wooden spoons. "We are seven brothers and one sister" explained Berthou. He also had an old butter churn, the type with a hole in the top in which was placed a thick stick. The only place I had seen a similar churn was in St Fagan's Folk Museum near Cardiff. In addition to his antique furniture and various gadgets from bygone days he was also the proud owner of a fine collection of old books in French and Breton, as well as a number of school photographs from around 1900 with all the children in traditional costume.

It is unusual to meet an old man whose delight in the things of his youth was so evident. Jean Berthou retained his heritage, allowing it to live in his home.

Trips to the Isles

It might be difficult to believe, but there was once a Johnny who went all the way to sell onions on Orkney and Shetland. When Joseph Corre first went to the islands in 1925 with his father he was only 13 years old. But he was already experienced in his trade having spent two or three seasons apprenticeship in Aberdeen. Then in 1925 his father, who spent a total of 48 seasons on the islands decided it was time for his son to get to know the customers of the most northerly patch of all for the Roscoff onion-sellers.

With seven or eight large hampers each containing 260 kilos of onions, he went with his father to Kirkwall and Stromness on Pomona, the largest island on Orkney. The routine was to spend six weeks there and then return to Aberdeen for a fresh load of onions before sailing to Lerwick, the main island of Shetland. It would take him about a month to sell that load before going back again to Aberdeen.

"I used to keep my onions in a warehouse used by other onion-men in Aberdeen" he explained. "There was a man there who did the stringing for me. I only called twice every season on my customers and when I walked down the streets or through the country-side people would come out of the houses and run after me. I had no one to compete with me so I charged a little more than my colleagues on the mainland for the onions. I remember in 1935 there were 25 of us in the same company in Aberdeen with a total of 400 tons to sell but I was the only one going out to the islands. We would start from Roscoff in July and get home around Christmas, althought I spent Hogmanay on the islands many times". He could boast of having sold

106

onions in John O'Groats and he recalled having to make the crossing from Thurso to Stromness in a gale. Another of his memories of those northern islands was being able to read a newspaper at midnight in July.

When the Second World War began his father stayed on for a while to sell what remained of the onions while Joseph returned home to fight. He spent five years as a prisoner of war near Hamburg. After the war he did not return to the islands but settled down to make a living on his small-holding overlooking the sea at Pen-ar-lan on the outskirts of Roscoff growing onions, carrots and tomatoes. I noticed the little black onion seeds drying in the sun in front of the house but he said that his son did most of the work now.

He talked of what he ate when he was on Orkney and Shetland. For breakfast he had eggs, bacon and porridge, for lunch, beef and potatoes, a biscuit and cup of tea for tea and something similar for supper.

But it would be more colourful to quote his original Scots, ''Beef 'n' tatees, copotee 'n' a biscuit''. Joseph Corre is a small, wiry man, reminiscent of an island crofter ekeing out a slender living from fishing a rough sea and scraping the thin soil of an equally rough hinterland. He talks with amazing rapidity in a strong Scottish accent pronouncing the name of his adopted land as Sgotland with a soft consonant every time. Like many other former onion-sellers he still enjoyed the habits he had learnt in Scotland – playing darts and rings and insisting on his afternoon cup of tea.

*   *   *

Claude Tanguy has named his house Ballerno. He explained that Ballerno is a small town near Edinburgh on the road to Lanark adding that people who live there are both very kind and pleasant. I felt sure that the people of Ballerno would be delighted to hear that their favourite onion man had honoured them in this way.

Claude Tanguy retired from selling onions in 1975 after an operation; then two years later he returned to Scotland for a holiday. He immediately called on one of his former colleagues who was still selling onions in Edinburgh and asked if he could have a load to sell. Then, with time to do as he wished he returned to the streets where his former customers lived. "This time I could afford the time to accept the cup of tea, the whisky or the glass of wine or port I had been refusing over the years. When I was selling onions for real, it was always a problem how to refuse all this kindness. If I accepted a drink in one house the ones I had refused were sure to hear of it and would then be asking me "What's the matter with me?" They could get quite cross with me". But by returning to Edinburgh for a holiday he sold some onions for his friend and had all the time in the world to enjoy a drink and a gossip with all his former customers without offending anyone.

A few weeks before my conversation with Claude Tanguy he had met two youths, both wearing kilts, in Roscoff. He went to talk to them and immediately one of them said "You're the man who used to sell onions to my mother". Tanguy took them home and gave them supper – they had been having difficulty in finding somewhere to stay and the previous night both had slept under a boat on the beach in Carantec. They stayed with him for a week.

Claude Tanguy is a short, powerful and kindly man with thick, slightly greying hair. He is obviously a person who is ready to do a favour for anyone. The day I talked to him he had been helping to fill sacks with onions for three Johnnies who at that time were selling onions in Leith. A lorry would be leaving with a load of onions for Leith the following week. "They're selling well this year. There's no competition you see. I remember 110 onion Johnnies in 1935-6. In those days thousands of Johnnies were going to Britain; this year only 34 have paid for a membership card of the *Association des vendeurs d'oignon*". He told me that 15,000 onion sellers used to come to Britain at one time but according to all the figures I had discovered I could only assume that this figure was the total number of migrating Johnnies for a number of seasons, if not for the whole of the inter-war period. It's very difficult to know how accurate any of these figures might be, particularly in the years before the *Association* was established. And by the time the *Association* had been formed the onion trade was in decline.

Claude Tanguy started selling onions in 1928 at the age of 13. "There were many big families around here in those days and if you could arrange for some of the boys to go away to England to sell onions, well, that was a few bellies fewer to fill. One old Johnny was telling me last week how his little brother had wandered on to an onion boat while they were loading and while he was still on board the ship sailed! He was away from home for six months! Mind you, it was a bloody hard life. We never worked on Sundays but we had to make up for the time when we weren't working.

We had to get up at a quarter past midnight on the Monday morning to string onions as we hadn't done any on Sunday! Fair play though, the bosses were very hard on themselves too. Many times I remember walking twenty miles one way with a load of onions on my back or pushing a wheelbarrow full of onions. More than once the police stopped me at night because I had no light on the barrow! But on the whole we were on good terms with the police. They often came round to the warehouse for a cup of tea". Like Joseph Corre he pronounced it 'copatee' and spoke excellent English with a strong Scottish accent.

They had no difficulty in getting warehouses in those days. "I remember Peta Claude telling me that he would rent a warehouse for five or six months a year and take the key home with him to Roscoff. Nobody would be using the storehouse for the rest of the year" he said.

Claude Tanguy's favourite relaxation when in Scotland was to go and watch Hibernian Football Club, although he would always be out selling onions after the match. "But in the latter years, selling onions had become very easy. We could sell to every house without any difficulty. Sometimes at the end of the afternoon I would be on my way back to the warehouse with just a few strings on the bike which I would be keeping for some of my faithful customers. Then someone would run after me or a car would stop – I couldn't refuse to sell to anyone but I never liked to disappoint my regular customers".

His children were also very fond of Scotland. His son had been with him selling onions in Ballerno and his three daughters had been there working as *au pairs* at the same time on more than one occasion. On the wall in his lounge was a

109

painting of an Edinburgh street with the castle in the background, the work of John Fielder.

It was a picture of which he was proud. Claude Tanguy was equally proud of his collection of malt whiskies but since my appreciation of the national drink of Scotland didn't match his we settled for a *calvados*. Afterwards we said goodbye and I left his pleasant house in *Kernaguer*.

The popularity of the onion-sellers cannot be questioned. In addition to his much loved onions the Johnny brought with him a little exotic colour as well. His distinctiveness was almost as much a part of his attraction as the tasty and useful onions he offered his buyers. When Vincent Cabioch fell to his death in Roscoff in January 1973, his picture and a report was carried in the *South Wales Echo*. When Claude Deridon returned to Porthmadog for a holiday in 1977 the women of Port and Cricieth ran out of their houses to embrace and kiss him – it was some indication of his popularity. It would be difficult to blame the women for displaying such affection, Deridon even with his eightieth birthday approaching was still a tall and handsome man.

François Gueguen, who wandered so restlessly around the old port of Roscoff, first told me about Deridon. The first time I called to see him his wife said he was in bed, he had been out fishing early that morning and was very tired. Gueguen had told me that Deridon had had a serious heart operation and I gathered that his heart relied on a pace-maker. I called again two or three times without any luck. Then, one fine afternoon, I saw Gueguen sitting on a bench on the far end of the old port of Roscoff, a corner called Pen Al Leur, accompanied with two or three others. Among them I recognized Deridon, since another former Johnny had shown me a picture of him a few days earlier.

I walked over to join them and was welcomed warmly. There, with the warm afternoon September sun on our backs and Porz Glaz behind us we talked about Porthmadog, Cricieth and Wimbledon.

Deridon had started selling onions in Wimbledon in 1920 when he was 16 years old with, according to his own evidence, a scant knowledge of French and no English. Before starting in

110

Claude Deridon

the onion trade he had been a farm labourer in the Roscoff area. He settled easily and happily into the life of an onion-seller in Wimbledon and some of his children went over with him for the annual migration. And it was to Wimbledon that he returned every Autumn until 1939. After the war he decided to try a different area and went to Porthmadog. His father had been selling onions in Porthmadog in his youth and according to Claude he spoke Welsh fluently. The Johnnies were restrained from selling in their traditional manner in 1947, so it was in 1948 that Claude Deridon settled in to the business of selling onions around the northern end of Cardigan Bay. For many years he hired a ship which sailed directly from Roscoff to Porthmadog with the onions and the onion-men. But in his final years the onions would be brought over in a lorry which crossed on the Roscoff-Plymouth ferry.

Although his father spoke Welsh fluently Claude Deridon's knowledge of the language was just about sufficient to sell his onions – he was probably too old to assimilate another language thoroughly by the time he started coming to Wales. Nevertheless, he knew a lot of useful phrases:

> 'Sut dach chi?' (How are you?)
> 'Da iawn'. (Very Well)
> 'Dach chi isho nionod?' (Do you want onions?)
> 'Dim ishe heddiw, digon i gael, dewch tro nesa. Dach chi ishe paned o de?' (Don't want any today, got plenty, call next time. Do you want a cup of tea?)
> 'Dwi isho dim. Cael un tro nesa'. (I don't want anything. I'll have one next time).

Although his knowledge of the Welsh language was obviously limited, he spoke those phrases in beautiful dialect. I had tried to locate a retired onion man whom I had been told spoke North Welsh fluently.

His name was François Danielu and according to what I had been told he first came to Caernarfon in the twenties and spent the rest of his working life selling onions around Caernarfon and Bangor. Unfortunately, I failed to find him. It would have been interesting to see how well he would have been able to converse in Welsh with someone like Joseph Olivier, who had made Newcastle Emlyn, Dyfed his base and who spoke the dialect of that area with all its lovely eccentricities.

112

Claude Deridon (right) in Cricieth with one of his colleagues, Jean Guivac'h (centre). Also in the picture is another Breton, Yves Hervé, who was manager of the Prince of Wales Hotel in the town.

Claude Deridon (second left back row) with his wife and other members of the family in Porthmadog a few years after the war. The boy in the front row is his son.

Deridon talked with nostalgia of 7, Pen-cei, Porthmadog where he lived during the selling season, and where he would string onions in the open air during warm September evenings – in surroundings not unlike those in which we talked on that afternoon in Roscoff. It was easy to see how he could dream about his old friends in Porthmadog in such a place.

It was with great sadness that I heard of his death in 1986.

The Singer

Saik Mevel is well known among the onion men as 'Le Chanteur'. During the years he spent selling onions in London he used to supplement his earning by singing in *cabarets* in the West End. Saik Mevel knew a large number of ballads and folk songs from the Roscoff area and he sang one of the Johnnies songs, the English/Breton bilingual song 'Good onions, very cheap', but in the London *cabarets* he would sing such songs as 'For you alone' and 'Your tiny hand is frozen' for which he would earn £5 a night. Mevel was born in 1899 and when I talked to him he was approaching his eightieth birthday, yet his voice was still strong and clear as a bell and showed that here was a trained singer, a disciplined singer. He named his old singing teacher, evidently a respected person in the Roscoff area. "He taught me to sing with my head, not my heart".

He sang 'Bro Goz va Zadou', Brittany's national anthem, which is an adaptation of Wales's anthem 'Land of my Fathers' and is sung to the same tune. "I love watching Wales playing rugby – on the television" he said "so that I can hear the crowd sing that song at the start of the match. And I can join in and sing until the windows rattle". He tried another song which I assumed to be a Breton version of 'Cartref' (Home), a popular Welsh song of the inter-war period. But he had great difficulty in remembering the tune and I only disgraced the reputation of a musical nation with my pitiful voice as I tried ot help. Nevertheless, I was confident that the song he was trying to sing was 'Cartref', of which a Breton version under the title 'Va zi bihan' (My Little House) exists.

Then another voice broke into song in the room – a crystal clear soprano. This was Saik Mevel's daughter who had

115

Armistice Day in Porthmadog and Claude Deridon (centre of picture with beret) marches with his Welsh friends.

obviously inherited the talents of her father. I asked if she also sang publicly as her father had done.

She replied that she was a member of the local folk group 'Mouez Rosko' (The Voice of Roscoff) whose name I had seen on countless posters around the town. 'Mouez Rosko' is a traditional folk group who specialize in singing the folk songs of the area – some of them songs they had learnt from Saik Mevel himself. She added, with some pride, that the old man was also a poet and sometimes wrote Breton words for them to sing to traditional tunes.

But music and poetry are not the only things which give pleasure to Saik Mevel. He is proud of a picture of London Bridge which hangs in his lounge – a copy of a picture by Bernard Buffet. But he is a lot prouder of a still life painting by Cecil Kennedy which he had received from the artist himself. "In every picture by Kennedy you will find a ladybird in some corner or other. I sold onions to Kennedy for many years – he was one of my best customers".

Saik Mevel began selling onions in 1913, at the age of 14, with his father in Grimsby. The following year he was about to sail again when war broke out and he was stopped from crossing to England, just in time. He took his trade up again in 1923, in Croydon this time, and from then until 1939 his customers were the people of London and the vast suburbs. "At that time, there were more than 150 Johnnies in London, Essex and Surrey alone" he said. Even in the early seventies, he believed that there were around 50 onion sellers operating in the South-East. After the Second World War he concentrated his selling on Romford and Hornchurch and he is now adamant that the finest people in the world live in Essex. He came over for the last time in 1974.

Like many others Mevel was here when war was declared in 1939. "I was selling onions in Leytonstone and I was ordered to return home immediately. I joined the fire brigade in Paris and that's where I stayed until the end of the war".

As we said our farewells in that narrow street behind Roscoff's Notre Dame Croaz Baz Church, I noticed that he had named his house 'Summerfield'. It seemed somehow an appropriate name for the house of a man who had spent so

117

Claude Deridon and a colleague demonstrate that it is possible to ride a bike even when overloaded with onions.

118

much of his life in that most English corner of England.

The Welsh Johnnies of Dossen

I have already said a number of times that so many onion Johnnies spoke and behaved almost exactly like their customers. Joseph Olivier was another perfect example of this tendency. Joseph had a small farm in a hamlet called Mecheroux, less than two kilometres from Dossen. Olivier Bertevas had first told me about him. "I don't think he had much English", Bertevas had told me. "When we were crossing and going through the customs into England some official would tell us something and every time Joseph would be asking me "What did he say now?" All I know is that he would sell a lot of onions in the farms and villages around Newcastle Emlyn".

After making a number of enquiries in Dossen, I was directed towards Joseph Olivier's farm. I arrived as he and his son Michel, another former onion-man, were coming out of the house after lunch. "Good afternoon, sir, how are you?" I said to him in Welsh, my best South Cardiganshire Welsh.

"Very well boy, where do you come from?" he replied. It was a thrilling experience, hearing those words spoken in the beautiful Dyfed dialect in such a remote corner of Brittany. I told him what I had come for and he gave a very straight answer. "I'm behind with the cauliflower harvest, the only free time I have is on Sunday. Come to see me on Sunday and we can talk".

As the following Sunday was to be the last of my stay in Brittany I had arranged to spend the day with friends and I told him so.

But politely yet firmly, like many an old farmer I knew from Cardiganshire and Pembrokeshire, he refused to budge an inch. "What if I come rather late one evening?" I offered. The answer was still the same. "We work till nine every night and then I'll be too tired to talk. Come on Sunday". Again, like many a Dyfed farmer I knew, there was no great gushing welcome – he was a little suspicious of me and made no attempt to hide the fact. He even looked like a farmer from that part of Wales – the Celtic shape of the head with a broad bald furrow down the

119

centre. And then there was Michel. With his head lowered his foot toyed with a pebble in the sandy ground.

I finally agreed and said that I would come on Sunday. "I'll come about five o'clock" I said. "Alright, come to the café in Dossen by five" he replied. "But there are three cafés in Dossen" I said. I had noticed two and assumed that there must be another which I had not seen. "Come to the one which sells tobacco" I was told. We were about to say goodbye when he asked "Where in Cardiganshire do you come from?". "Tregaron" I replied, "did you go up there?". "Michel would go there after François Kergoat stopped going to Lampeter". "Do you remember the names of some of the farms around Tregaron?" I asked Michel. "No, I don't remember their names now but I could still find my way around them. I went round them all' he replied. In the presence of his father Michel was prepared to speak only when spoken to. He was behaving like scores of farmers' sons in Cardiganshire or Pembrokeshire would have done in that situation.

Just as I had suspected the lunch at Kerlouan on the following Sunday was extremely pleasant and it proved difficult for me to extract myself from the conversation and company. It was almost quarter to six by the time I arrived at the Café-Tabac in Dossen. In the café it was standing room only and I could see no sign of Joseph Olivier anywhere around the packed tables.

Then I heard a voice "Where have you been, then, lad?". The man who spoke to me in Welsh was hardly recognisable as the Joseph Olivier I had met a few days earlier on his farm in Mecheroux. He was neatly dressed and wore a beret concealing a bald head which had been so prominent before. I bought a bottle of red wine and went over to talk to Joseph and his friends. "What time is it now?" he asked in mock innocence, typical of the gentle leg pulling of the Cardiganshire farmers I remember so well. "I think it's about half past five" I lied lamely. "And when did you say you would be here?". He enjoyed persevering with his joke. I apologized profusely and explained about my lunch. "After all" I protested, "we had *Kig ha Farz*, * it wouldn't have been proper to rush that". A dreamy, slightly envious look came into his eyes. "*Kig ha Farz*. I wish I had been with you. I haven't had a meal of *Kig ha Farz* for

120

Michel Olivier and his father, Joseph, outside their farmhouse in Mecheroux. Joseph did all his selling from Newcastle Emlyn.

years. We don't have it around these parts any longer".

Gradually we got around to talking about his childhood. "There were eight of us children and plenty to do to get something with which to fill our bellies – usually potatoes. They were hard days, when I was young, potatoes for dinner, potatoes for supper and if we were lucky, a little bit of bacon to go with it. We had plenty of bread, mind, we used to eat ten times as much bread in those days as we do now. We had two or three cows and would rear two or three pigs a year. If you liked bacon it wasn't too bad, if you didn't it was just bad luck. It was only rarely, on Sundays, that we had fresh meat".

It was in that bleak era that Joseph Olivier in 1931 at the age of 12 went with his father to Newcastle Emlyn for the first time. "Since then the Welsh have fed me, given me clothes and always had an open door for me. I have often regretted that I stopped coming over to sell onions, the Welsh were such nice people. A lot of English people came to Newcastle Emlyn after the war and I remember that they couldn't pronounce names like Crymych and Abercuch, they used to say Crimick and Aberkick".

In the early years he would sail from Roscoff to Swansea with his onions, then to Portsmouth and finally in the last years before his final trip in 1974 he would cross from Roscoff to Plymouth. "And remember, next time you visit Newcastle Emlyn you must go to the Ivy Bush, Cawdor Hotel and The Three Compasses and remember me to them. I want you to thank them for me. I received a lot of kindness from them. If I couldn't pay the duty to bring my onions into the country any one of those pubs would lend me the money I needed. I always repaid them within a week but I've got a lot to thank them for. Then I used to stay in a farm called Cwrt Coed – we had a storehouse there – those poeple were the finest I ever met. I owe a great debt to Ben James of Cwrt Coed. He always said 'no' whenever I asked him for something but he relented every time. He never refused me anything. He, too, used to lend me money to pay the import duty".

He recalled having to appear in court in Newcastle Emlyn for driving their van without a licence. "I was caught by Constable Simon Davies. I was fined five shillings for driving the van and

122

* *Kig ha Farz* is a traditional Breton meal consisting of boiled pork and coarse oat flour – a meal of the rural, labouring class.

my father was fined five shillings for allowing me – ten shillings all together". He explained that he had been too young by a year to apply for a driving licence when that happened.

He listed the towns and villages where he would sell his onions – Cardigan, Fishguard, St. David's, Solva, Newport, New Quay, Brynberian, Crymych – but it was the Welsh forms of the names he used every time although the English forms are commonly used even by Welsh speakers. "Sometimes I would go into the heart of the Preseli mountains, the van would drop me near Brynberian and I would walk to the farms around the mountain and the van would pick me up on its way back. I often walked a mile from the road to a farm and a mile back to the road before going on towards another farm – I needed to make a good sale at those farms to make it worth all that walking. I used to sell three sizes of strings and fair play to the women on those farms, they always bought the largest ones".

When the war broke out Joseph Olivier had to return home, but he managed to sell all his remaining onions before departing. He went back to Brittany and then responded to de Gaulle's demand and sailed to Ouessant and from there to Birkenhead. He spent the war on ships sailing between Lisbon and Freetown, Gold Coast and Greenock.

I mentioned a poem by Isfoel, the celebrated farmer-poet from the 'Cilie' farm, Llangrannog. The poem described the war coming and there was no Johnny Onions. Then the war ended and Johnny returned. What a welcome for the good news, he buys a string and enjoys a grand feast of boiled onions to celebrate Johnny's safe return.

"Would you have been that Johnny?" I asked. "I suppose so" he replied. "I used to go to the 'Cilie' and I remember Dafydd Jones (Isfoel was his bardic name) very well, and the one with the red hair. (The one with the red hair was Alun Jones, Isfoel's brother, also a very fine Welsh poet). I would go to the 'Cilie' to get reeds, too. That was one of the jobs we would do on Sunday. On Sunday mornings I would string onions and in the afternoons I would go with my sickle to cut a load of reeds. Pay? No, the farmers were glad to get rid of it".

123

But did he not go to church on Sunday? "No, I haven't been in a church for years. I – how do they say – I think a lot of the Creator but not much of the 'Father' ".

He talked of the numbers of onion-sellers who were based in that part of Cardiganshire, Pembrokeshire and Carmarthenshire. "When the war broke there were 14 Johnnies in Newcastle Emlyn – not all of them working for the same company. And François Kergoat had 10 men working for him in Lampeter. Kergoat had his storehouse in a pub on the square in Lampeter. That building is a bank now.

"I have often regretted that I have stopped selling onions, especially to the Welsh. A lot of English poeple came to the Welsh countryside after the war, but the Welshman, he's like the Breton. I could get on with him. It's a great pity, but it doesn't pay to come over now. The cost of bringing the onions over is going up and the value of sterling is going down. If only it were worth my while I would be over there now".

Joseph and his friends then got up from the table and crossed the road to the other café to continue their drinking there. They had invited me to join them but a few minutes earlier my conversation with Joseph was interrupted by another former Johnny, Pierre Guivach, who used to hawk his onions in Swansea and the West Wales Industrial Valleys.

The typical South Wales valleys character has the reputation of being cheerful, witty, and extrovert with a short fuse but who can simmer down equally quickly. It is a description which could apply just as well to Pierre Guivach, or Peter the Johnny as he was known to his customers in Swansea, Llanelli and the surrounding villages. It was typical of Pierre that when he overheard me talking to Joseph Olivier he shouted from his position at the bar, "Do you know Llanelli, Swansea, Carmarthen? I sold onions in them all". I told him not to go away so that we could have a drink and a chat together in a few minutes, once I had finished with Joseph. He did not go away either, and were it not for numerous hints from the barmaid we could have been there for a week. Pierre was finding the *pression* very much to his liking and insisted, if I was to live up to the good name of the Welsh people, that I should carry on drinking with him.

Pierre Guivac'h, Peter the Johnny, with a barrow-load of carrots near his house in Dossen.

Some months after my conversation with Pierre I talked about him to a friend from Llanelli. "I remember Peter coming to Llangennech (a village outside Llanelli) before the war" my friend told me. "He spoke Welsh perfectly". But by the time I came across Pierre, he spoke very little Welsh.

The reason, no doubt, was that when he came over after the war he went to Newcastle-on-Tyne and Scotland. However, he could still repeat some of the Welsh phrases he used to sell onions when he was in the Welsh speaking villages of the Swansea valley.

Pierre came to Swansea for the first time with his father in 1921 when he was nine years of age. And it was to Swansea that he came for the following 17 years sailing from Roscoff almost every year on the *Iris* – a ship that sank with a load of coal near Île de Batz on a return journey a few years before the war. "About 60 of us would come over on sailing boats, three or four ships coming together" he said.

He obviously had a great regard for the Welsh although there had been difficult times. There was the 'Buy British' movement which he said had affected the Johnnies.

"Some people wouldn't look at us but others just accepted the fact that we were in Wales and we had a job to do. And they would buy from us. Then there was the time of the General Strike when life was tough and some people weren't pleased to see us". He lit another *Gitanes* and coughed fiercely; Pierre even coughed with the committment of an old collier "Oh, yes, I could get on well with the Welsh" he added. "But, we're all Welsh, well, all Celts, anyway. It was only on one occasion that I ever had any trouble. I was nine years old and having my mid-day soup at the Strand in Swansea when a policeman came to me. I remember that he was from Fforest Fach. He said I was too naughty and cheeky for a nine year old. Well, I may have been cheeky but I was never naughty".

Pierre was in Swansea when the war began and he had to return immediately to Brittany. He had a younger brother in the company who was too young to be called up and it was that brother who stayed on in Swansea to sell the remaining onions. Pierre was taken prisoner of war near Dunkirk and spent the war in P.O.W. camps in Breslav, Poland. He learnt German

126

very rapidly and was soon fluent in Polish too and as a result got work as a translator.

"The Germans used to tell me that they would have Churchill cleaning out the stables in Germany after the war. I would answer that when the war was over Hitler would be digging for coal in a South Wales coal-mine. They didn't like that. I don't like the Germans. One reason why I don't go to sell onions now is the fucking Jerries – they got my legs. That's why I can't talk to them today. I can talk to the young ones, but never the old ones".

In spite of the fact that he never had a day's formal schooling in his life, Pierre is obviously a remarkable linguist. He spoke five languages fluently and evidently at one time also spoke Welsh fairly well. "The reason why I can speak these languages? I never turned my back on my first language – Breton – and here in Dossen, in the sound of that language, I have spent the greater part of my life".

I asked him if he knew anything about the *Hilda* disaster. "My father had intended to sail on that boat but he had some onions left over and decided to stay another day in Southampton to sell them" said Pierre. I failed to get confirmation of his story but it was certainly very interesting. Pierre added that the *Hilda's* mast had been left near the scene of the disaster for many years and he had actually seen it himself in 1921.

After the war, Pierre returned to his former trade. "I went first to Newcastle, but I never really got on with the Geordies so I went to Aberdeen the following year", he recalled. "When I was in Swansea the Welsh would tell me that they didn't like the Scots. Well, I got on very well with them all – Scots and Welsh. But I never trusted the Geordies. When I was in Swansea I used to sell onions to a Professor in the University – his name was Diveres*; later when I went to Aberdeen I met his son who was a lecturer in that University".

Pierre remained in Aberdeen until he retired in 1974.

By now the cafe was empty except for Pierre, myself and the youthful barman, who was son of the owners. Every so often his mother came in and grumbled something about closing time. "Don't take any notice of her, hell, I'm a bloody good customer" was Pierre's response to my suggestions that we

127

* Diveres was in fact a Breton and a notable Celtic scholar.

might take the hint. He insisted that we both had another half of the *pression*. Pierre turned to the son. "Your father was a Johnny too". The youth denied it and a fierce argument followed until the father was called into settle the dispute. The father said that he had never sold onions but had been a fisherman and often used to sail from Brittany to some of the Cornish ports – so it was easy to see how Pierre had been mistaken. No sooner had one argument been settled then another flared up – a matter of nationality and of belonging. "Je suis Breton et fier d'être Breton, mais je suis aussi Francais" was the cafe owner's opinion on the matter, an attitude which got no sympathy from the fiery Pierre – he was a Breton and the French version of the two finger sign showed what he thought of France – adding that that anyway was what France thought of Brittany. The argument raged back and forth for another half an hour and by the time we left, the houses were all shuttered up for the night and leaving a trail of *Gitanes* smoke behind him he wobbled uncertainly home on his old bike.

Nothing else moved in that dark and shadowy street. It was hard to believe that this little man was 68 years of age but it was not difficult to believe that he had been selling onions in Swansea, Port Talbot, Llanelli, Llangyfelach, Gorseinon and the Swansea Valley. He was certainly one of them.

While I had been talking earlier that afternoon to Joseph Olivier an old man at the other end of the table had said a few words to me in Welsh. I had made a note that I would have to talk to him later but that was before I met Pierre Guivach. As a result I returned a few days later to Dossen to try to find him. I called at Joseph Olivier's house to make some inquiries.

Joseph was not at home. He was picking carrots in the fields, but since his wife was going there shortly to help him I waited to give her a lift in my car. She gave me a glass of wine, tidied up a little and put on her clogs and in a while we left with the large *ki bleiz* (alsatian) racing furiously after us through the narrow lane until we got to the field which was almost in the middle of Dossen. It took quite a long time for Joseph to establish who I wanted to meet. With his heel he drew a diagram in the soil. "You and I were sitting here, the sailor was sitting here, my cousin was sitting there, I don't remember who

128

Jean-Marie Guivac'h, brother of Pierre, one of Dossen's "Welsh" Johnnies. He sold his onions in Carmarthen, Newcastle Emlyn, Aberystwyth, and then in Scotland.

was sitting in that corner..." In the end I realised that the man I wanted to talk to was in fact Joseph's cousin and that he had been selling onions in Newcastle Emlyn between 1928 and 1939. He could still speak Welsh quite fluently, like his cousin he spoke the distinctive dialect of North Pembrokeshire and South Cardiganshire and praised his former customers in Crymych and New Quay. He had spent the war years imprisoned in Austria and he never returned again to Wales although he still longed sometimes for the happy company of the bar-room of the Red Cow in Newcastle Emlyn. "When I was young I could speak Welsh as well as you but I've forgotten a lot of it by now".

We could so easily have forgotten that we were in this remote corner of Brittany. We could have been in Llangrannog or some other seaside village in Cardiganshire or Pembrokeshire. A car could be driven onto the beach; there was an island a little way out to sea and it was evidently inhabited. The land showed signs of cultivation and smoke came from the chimney of an old farmhouse. At low tide I suspected it would have been possible to walk across to the island but on that day the tide was in and a stiff breeze sent the "white horses" chasing each other across the bay. We could have been talking outside the Pentre Arms in Llangrannog. After all, were we not conversing in the very dialect one would expect to hear in Llangrannog? But there were other signs which quickly dispelled the illusion, the *Kanterbrau* advertisement, the *Salle de jeux* and *Les Dunes*, the windows with shutters and Yves Madec's fishery business.

I said goodbye to Jean-Marie Olivier after promising that I would be back in a year's time to share a bottle of wine on a Sunday afternoon with him and Joseph in the "café where they sell tobacco". I stopped briefly to shake hands with Joseph in his carrot field and to promise that I would convey his best wishes to his many friends in West Wales and to reiterate the goodbye which no one had believed when he had said it himself in 1974.

Onion-seller in Swansea.

Some songs and ballads of the onion men

Good onions, very cheap,
Prenit ognon mat
Digant ar Roskoad.
Good onions, very cheap,
Prenit ognon mat
Digant ar Breizad.

Johnniget an ognon
Zo deut euz abell-bro
Da werza d'ar Zaozon
Gwella vouen ognon 'zo
Da lakat er zouben
Pe gant eun tam rata
Pe gant eur fritaden
Er podig da gana.

Skuiz-maro vont bemdez
Da redet an hentchou
O sevel en tiez
Da skei war an doriou.
Hor c'hein a zo kignet
Dindan ar zam pounner
Hag hor chupen toullet
Zo mat d'ar pilhaouer.

Echuet hon deg leo
Dindad peb amzer fall
E klevomp en distro
Ar Mestr o fraonval.
Ha pa zaimp d'an daoulin
Ha da sonjal pedi
Pe d'an offern vintin
E kwezimp war hor fri,

Prenit 'vit ma c'hellem
Kas d'ar vugaligou
D'ar ger pa zistroimp
Kountellou, muzikou,
Prenit 'vit ma lako
Mylady Marijan
Thé Saoz ken a foeltro
Da virvi war an tan.

Translation

Good onions, very cheap,
Buy good onions.

132

From the Roscovite;
Good onions, very cheap,
Buy good onions
From the Breton.

Johnny Onions
Came from a distant land
To sell to the English
Onions which are the finest
For putting in the soup
Or on the grill if you wish
Or in the frying pan
Or in the pot to sing.

Dead tired they'll be daily
Trudging the roads
Stopping by the houses
To knock the doors.
Their backs are raw
Beneath their heavy loads
Their coats are torn
And fit for the rag-man.

Finishing our ten miles
In all sorts of filthy weather
And hearing when we return
The boss complaining.
And when we go on our knees
And turn to our prayers
or go to the morning Mass
We could sleep on our noses.

Buy so that I may
Take home to my children
When I return
Toys for counting, toys for music
Buy so that
Milady Marian
Can rush the tea from England
And boil it on the fire.

*

Paotred Rosko

N'eus par, e Breiz Izel da baotred Rosko,
Brudet 'int 'vit o nerz dre-holl 'barz ar vro,
Diwallit da goueza dindan o fao,
Ro-sko, sko mibin, sko kallet, sko atao!

133

Ouspenn, labourerien dispar int ivez,
Da c'houlou-deiz 'maint er maez eus o gwele.
Gwelit o bemdez en aochou tro war dro,
Kerkent ma vo tre, betek ma vo lano,
O pelhiat bezin war ar reier garo,
Rosko, sko mibin, sko kalet, sko atao!

Kalz ijin o deus ivez paotred Rosko,
Eus Bro-C'hall a bez o deus graet an dro,
'Vit gwerza o zrevad dre ar marc'hajo,
Rosko, sko mibin, sko kalet, sko atao!
Dre Baris, dre Vro-Zaoz o deus tremenet,
Mont a raint hebale betek penn ar bed.
Ar Roskoad, gant e vouez skiltr a youc'ho;
"Patatez, brikoli, ougnon, articho!
"Didabit, kemerit, an neb a garo"
Rosko, sko mibin, sko kalet, sko atao.

N'eus ket lorc'husoc'h eget paotred Rosko,
Gwalenn war o biz, c'houez vat war o bleo.
Voulouzenn ledan en dro d'ho zog kolo,
Rosko, sko mibin, sko kalet, sko atao.
Gant o dousig pa'z eont d'ar pardoniou,
'Kargont he godell a bep seurt madigou
Anaout a reont mad kement dans a zo
Ar ganaouenn ivez 'blij eston d'ezo
Evelse ar merc'hed 'zo pitilh ganto
Rosko, sko mibin, sko kalet, sko atao!

Translation

The Lads of Roscoff

There are no equals in lower Brittany, to the lads of Roscoff,
Celebrated for their strength throughout the land,
Take care you do not fall into their hands
*Rosko, sko mibin, sko kalet, sko atao!
Untiring workers are they who
At the crack of dawn are out of their beds,
Daily you'll see them around the shores
As soon as the tide is out, until it returns
They comb the seaweed from the rocks
Rosko, sko mibin, sko kalet, sko atao.

Many a guile have the lads of Roscoff,
Through the whole of France have they wandered,
In the markets they peddled their produce,

134

Rosko, sko mibin, sko kalet, sko atao!
Through Paris, through England have they tramped,
They'll go to the corners of the world without hesitation
Shouting hoarsely, the lads of Roscoff;
"Potatoes, broccoli, onions, artichokes,
Choose, take, anyone who wishes".
Rosko, sko mibin, sko kalet, sko atao.

There are none prouder than the lads of Roscoff,
Rings on their fingers, hair slicked in its place
A wide band of velvet around their straw hats,
Rosko, sko mibin, sko kalet, sko atao.
With a sweetheart each goes to the Pardons
Filling her pockets with sweet things;
Well do they know every dance
And the songs, too, which will please her,
No wonder the girls all love them.
Rosko, sko mibin, sko kalet, sko atao.

*This line cannot be adequately translated since it relies on a pun on the name Rosko (which is the Breton form of Roscoff). Here the name is taken to mean "Strike a blow". Literally, therefore, the whole line translates, "Strike a blow, a swift blow, a hard blow, a regular blow".

*

La Vie de Johnnoy

Le jour d'été qu'ils sont partis
Sur un batiment lesté à Rosko,
L'air heureux, on vit les Johnnies
Rire à travers leurs chansons
Et lancer aux gens un gai kenavo.
Pour cinq ou six mois très loin ils vont,
Sans trop de bile les attendrons
Et voilà la vie du pauvre cher Johnny.

Au pays saxon à peine arrivés
Et du bâtiment finie la décharge,
Ills s'en vont, un bâton grevé
D'oignons meurtrissont l'épaule,
Sans arrêt, sur les chemins en marge,
Trottant, fourbus, la chair morte,
Tombant parfois, faisant la chine aux portes...
Et voilà la vie du pauvre cher Johnny.

Et quand le paquet, par malheur,
Passé midi n'est pas vendu,

De leurs yeux coulent des pleurs,
Cars les épaules sont moulues,
Que les oignons ne sont-ils des oranges!
On n'aurait pas tout un jour debattu,
Sans manger, cette marchandise étrange!
Et voilà la vie du pauvre cher Johnny!

Qu'importe le temps, allez, en route!
Que le vent rage ou bien qu'il pleuve!
On dormira tard quoi qu'il en coûte,
Et de bonne heure la couchette sera veuve.
Courage! c'est bientôt la France
Et le retour! En haut les coeurs!
La peine est finie. O douce créance!
Et voilà la vie du pauvre cher Johnny!

Translation

The Life of the Johnny

On the summer's day when they departed
On a ship loaded in Roscoff
Joyful of spirit were the Johnnies
Bellowing and laughing their songs,
Throwing to their friends a gay 'kenavo'.
They go for five or six long months
With little comfort to await them,
And that's the life of the poor dear Johnny.

In the land of the English, no sooner do they arrive
And the ship has been unloaded
Then they're away, the loaded stick
Of onions bruising their shoulders,
Non-stop, along the road-sides,
Trotting, tripping, senseless with weariness,
Sometimes falling, peddling from door to door...
That's the life of the poor dear Johnny.

And when there are strings, alas,
Still unsold after mid-day
The tears run from their eyes
Because their shoulders are bruised.
O that the onions were not oranges!
One would not have to slave all day
Without food, selling this strange merchandise!
That's the life of the poor dear Johnny.

Don't heed the weather, go on your journey,
Let the wind rage or the rain pour!

Late to bed, whatever the price
And early in the morning widowed is the bed.
Courage! before long, France,
And home! And a happy heart!
The pain is over, Sweet the reward!
And that's the life of the poor dear Johnny.

Guerz an *Hilda*

(C'huec'h ugent den beuzet e kichen Sant-Malo, en ho mesk pevar ugent
Breton deuz Leon).

An heur-waleur siouaz a zo
Atao, bepred o vont en dro
Hag o skei bemdez heb paouez
N'eur c'horn bennag war an dud kez.

Ne glever mui o komzeal
Nemet cuz a zarvoudou fall
Euz ar gwal heuriou a erru
Atao bemdez en tu pe du.

Ar vech-ma siouaz tud hor bro
Zo skoet heb truez d'ho zro
Gnt eun darvoud ar spountussa
A zo bet guelet dre ama.

D'an driouec'h devez a viz Du
E kreiz an noz tenval ha du
Al lestr *Hilda* tont deuz Bro-Zaoz
Zo bet beuzet e-kreiz an noz.

Ha warnez-hi kant tregont den
Akuipaj ha beachourien
Beuzet holl siouaz nemet c'houec'h
Heb sikour ebet deuz neb lec'h.

N'ho mesk pevar ugent Breizad
Euz Kastel-Pol ha Plouescat,
Euz Kleder, Treflez ha Rosko
Hag ar paressiou tro war-dro.

Ar re-man oa kustum bep bloaz
Da vont a vandennadou braz
Da Vro-Zaoz da verza ognon
A zo kalz e kostez Leon.

137

Hag e oant o tistrei d'ar ger
Laouen a galoun ha seder,
Mal braz warnez-ho da velet
Ho zud hag ho bro benniget.

Ne zonjen ket siouaz dez-ho
Oant vont var eon d'ar maro
Ha ne velijont mui ho zud kez
Araok ma golfont ho buhez!

Partiet d'ar guener d'an noz
Euz porz Southampton, euz Bro-Zaoz
Hint gle beza e Sant-Malo
D'an de warlerc'h gant al lano.

Mez d'ar zadorn vintin siouaz
Eun avel foll a zirollaz!
En eur zevel ar goagennou
Uz d'al lestr evel menesiou!

Houman e oa vel eur bluenn
Tol ha distol gant ar froadenn
Euz beg an eil goagen d'eben
Vel pa nije stur ebet ken.

Na re nemet bransigellet
Bepred war poent beza lounket
Ken dre all c'houeze an avel
Diwar zu douar Breiz-Izel.

Derc'hel mad reaz goulskoude
Penn d'an diroll epad an de,
Mes siouaz an noz a dosta
Hag ar mor a ia war voassa!

Ouspen-ze tre ma trosteaz
An danger ivez a greskaz
Abalmour d'ar c'herek zo
En dro da borz-mor Sant-Malo.

Ne oa mui evit douari
D'an heuriou oa gleet dezhi
O veza bet dalc'het re bell
E kreiz ar mor gant an avel.

Hag an noz teuaz warnezhi,
Eun an noz tenval e pehini
Ar glao, ar grizil, ar c'hrazac'h
Ar re ken du hag en eur zarc'h.

Ne oant ket 'vit guelet netra
En dro dezho 'vit ho hencha,

138

Sklerijen na tour-tan ebet
Vit gouzout dre belec'h monet!

Souden kein al lestr a stokaz
Euz eur garrek gant eun trouz braz,
Hag al lestr a c'harp n'eun tol krenn
En eur grena 'vel eun delienn!

Toullet siouaz gant ar roc'h-vor,
Ebarz n'he c'hreiz anter zigor,
An dour-mor a zaillaz ractal
War an dud kez en eur iudal!

Ar c'habiten laraz neuze:
''Na spountet ket en han' Doue,
Distaget ar bagou bihan
Ha tec'het warnezho buan!''

N'oa ket echuet he gomzou
Oant goloet gant ar goagennou!
Hag tud, lestr, ha bagou ieaz
Ractal da wouelek ar mor braz!

Eun neubeut c'hellaz gouskoude
Kemer eur vag, mez siouaz d'he,
Pe du monet, pe goste trei
Evit gallout n'em zavetei!

Rag ouspen ma ne velont ket
N'ouzont doare na c'hent ebet
Dre greiz ar mor hag araok pell
Siouaz dezho renkont mervel!

Eun neubeut all bignaz n'eur bern
Er beg huella duez eur wern
Pechini jome mez an dour
An esper iaffer d'ho zikour.

Mez an amzer a oa ken cri
Ken a skorne ho izili,
Hag kalz a gouezaz raog an de
Er mor an eil goud egile!

Lod all varvaz skornet, sklasset,
Hag jom a istribill bepred
Vel pa vijont bet en bue,
Na pebeuz maro didrue!

Antronoz vintin lestr *Ada*,
O vont da Vro-Zaoz dre ama,
Ho guel n 'eur blokad uz ar mour
Ha gas tud evit ho zikour!

139

Mez pebeuz heuz ha pebuez spont
N'ho deuz ket siouaz pa velont
E oa maro kalz anezho
Hag int a istribill atao!

C'houec'h hebken e oa he buhe:
Louis Rozec deuz Plouzevede,
Pol-Mari Penn, Jean-Louis Mouster
Ha Tanguy an Aot deuz Kleder.

Ollier Karoff deuz Rosko
Hag eur Zaoz, Grunsler he hano,
Pemp Breizad, hag an diveza
Kenta taner var an *Hilda*.

An *Ada* o c'hassaz ractal
Da Zant-Malo d'an hospital,
Ha ganthi neuze oa klevet
Ar c'helou truezuz meurbet!

Al lest *Hilda* korf ha madou
Beuzet war reer an Doriou
E kichen pors-mor Sant-Malo
Gant kant tregont den pe war-dro!

Deuz Sant-Malo ieaz neuze
Bagou er mor e peb koste
Da velet hen nijen kavet
Lod euz korfou ar re veuzet.

Mes, poulzet gant an avel foll
Ha gant ar goagennou diroll,
Ar c'horfou beuzet a ieaz
Pelloc'h, war-zu douar Sant-Cast.

Neuze ar mor evel skuizet
Euz ho derc'hel n'he zour sklasset
Ho distaolaz vel gant kounar
A bakadou war an douar!

Kri e oa an den na vouele
E Sant Cast an deveziou-se,
O velet an iliz karget
Digant korfou ar re veuzet!

O velet an iliz karget
Hag eur pez toul kreiz ar veret
Vit lakat ar re na vijen
Ket goulennet gant ho c'heren!

Kri ivez neb oa ket mantret,
O velet tud ar re veuzet

O n'em strinka war ar c'horfou
Hag ho guelc'hen gant ho daelou!

Krioc'h ve c'hoaz neb dremen-se
Dre vro Leon ma ne raffe
Eur zel a dru deuz ar paour-kez
Neuz mui den souten he vuhez!

Rag ped ha ped all n'ho deuz ket
Kollet eur mab, pe eur pried
Hag n'en doa siouaz nemet-ho
Evit gounit bara dezho!

Kolaik P.

Translation The Story of the *Hilda*

(One hundred and twenty men were drowned near St. Malo, among them 80 Bretons from the district of Leon).

The unfortunate hour sadly / Is for ever at work / Effecting daily / The lives of people somewhere or other.

One only hears talk / Of the bad events / Of the cruel hours which strike / Relentlessly here and there.

Sadly, on this occasion it was our people / Who were struck unmercifully / By the most terrible disaster / Ever seen in this land.

On the nineteenth day of November / In a black and dark night / The ship *Hilda* on its way from England / Was drowned in the middle of the night.

On the ship, a hundred and twenty men / Sailors and passengers / All were drowned except for six / Without assistance from anywhere.

Among them were eighty Bretons / From St. Pol and Plouescat / From Cleder, Treflez and Roscoff / And the neighbouring parishes.

These who would go annually / In a large crowd / To England to sell the onions / That are so plentiful in Leon.

They were returning home / Light hearted and happy / In a desperate hurry to see / Their famiies and their dear country.

Not one for a moment thought / That they were sailing to their death / And never again would they see their dear ones / Before they lost their lives.

On the Friday night they left / The port of Southampton in England / They should have been in St. Malo / The day after with the tide.

But on the morn of Saturday / A fierce wind arose / Whipping up the waves / like mountains above the ship.

141

The ship was like a feather / To be thrown and hurled by the currents / From the tip of one wave on to the next / As if it were rudder-less.

It only swayed / And all the time almost swallowed / So strongly blew the wind / From the direction of Lower Brittany.

However, it sailed onwards / In the teeth of the storm all day / But night was approaching / And the sea was getting rougher.

As well, as it approached / The danger was getting worse / Because of the rocks / In the vicinity of St. Malo.

It could not reach land / At the appointed hour / Having been delayed so long / By the wind while at sea.

The night came over them / A dark night with / Rain, hail, fog / Black as in a coffin.

They could see nothing / Around to guide them / no light or a lighthouse / To give their position!

Suddenly the bottom of the ship struck / on a rock with a terrible noise / Stopping instantly / Shaking like a leaf.

It was drilled by the rock / And split in half / And the water immediately broke / Over the screaming people!

Then the captain spoke: "Don't fear, in the name of God / Cast off the little boats / And flee in them instantly".

He had but spoken / When the waves washed over them! / And people, ship and boats went / Straight to the sea bed!

Some got to a boat / But unfortunately for them / Where would they go, in what direction / To save themselves!

If nothing could they see / They knew not what direction / Out to sea and in no time / Disaster for them, and death.

Some others climbed in a crowd / To the tip of the mast / Which remained above the water / Hoping it would be of help.

But so cruel was the weather / That their limbs froze / Many fell before the dawn / To the sea, one by one.

Others died of cold, frozen / And remained hanging there / As if they were still alive / Such a pitiless death!

The morning after, the *Ada*, / on its way to England, / Its sails a cluster above the waves / Brought men and assistance.

But such dismay and fear / Alas, when they found / So many dead / And still clinging to the mast!

Six only were still alive / Louis Rozec of Plouzevede, / Pol-Mari Penn, Jean-Louis Mouster / And Tanguy an Aot from Kleder;

142

Ollier Karoff from Roscoff / An Englishman called Grunsler (sic), / Five Bretons and the last / Was first stoker on the *Hilda*.

The *Ada* took them/To St Malo, to the hospital/And thus was told/The sad and terrible news.

The *Hilda*, body and belongings, / Was drowned on the Doriou rocks / Near the port of St. Malo / With a 130 men, or thereabouts.

But having been pushed by the fierce wind / And by the wild waves / The bodies were carried / Further, towards the land of St. Cast.

Then the sea, as if it had tired / Of keeping them in its freezing depths / Threw them in heaps / Fiercely on the beaches.

Cruel were those who did not weep / In St Cast on those days / From seeing the church full / Of the bodies of the drowned!

From seeing the church full / And the large hole in the graveyard / For burying those / Not sought after by loved ones.

Cruel, too, were those whose hearts were not broken / By the sight of the relatives of the drowned / Throwing themselves on the bodies / Washing them with their tears.

More cruel still were those who travelled / Through Leon and did not look / With pity at the one / With no one to give support in life.

Because large was the number of those / Who lost a son or husband / And who had but those / To win for them their bread.

*

Pense an *Hilda*

(E koun ar Vretoned o deuz kollet o buez ouz rec'hel Sant-Malo, e nosvez euzus ar zadorn, 18 a viz Du).
War don: Jezus, *Salver adorabl* pe *Silvestril*

Euz a Vro-Zaoz e teuent o bloaz ha laouen,
Yaouank an darn anezo, lod bugale zoken;
E kov al lestr tan *Hilda* e kanent an distro:
Euruz nep 'n eus ket ezom da vont kwit euz e vro!

Etre roched ha kroc'hen goazed, penn-a-vandenn
En o gouriz ler kaled a gloze aour melen,
An aour-ze hag a dlie trei lugern e beziou
E bevanz hag en eurvad da galz tiegeziou.

Rag edo deut evito koulz ar beilhadennou,
An diskwiz e korn an tan hag ar c'hontadennou;
Ha meur a hini yaouank a dride 'n eur zonjal
Edo evit an eured o douz oc'h o gedal.

143

E kreiz eun denvalijen ken du hag an ifern
E kroz mouez vraz an avel hag ar mor a dregern;
Ezel al lestr a orjel gant an tarziou: n'euz forz!
Eur sturier mad o deveuz hag ema tost ar porz.

Mez kerkent eur strakaden: Petra 'zo? Petra 'zo?...
Eur martolod a lavar 'n eur redeg 'biou d'ezo:
"Ar stur! aet eo kwit ar stur!" Hag an holl da devel,
Ar spount o kregi enno, hag an oll da zevel.

Al lestr paour a dec'h breman, distur, gant e frouden.
Ha da beleac'h o c'haso gant herr e redaden?
Euz e bost, ar c'habiten hen dinec'h da welet
A gemen eun dra bennag ha ne c'haller klevet.

Henvel ouz eun tenn kanol eur youc'haden a zao:
"Rec'hel! rec'hel an hon raog!" Kerkent, en dourbill c'hlao,
Eur stok spontuz ha safar hag an daouarn en oar,
Hag eur c'halvaden, unan, divent e kreiz ar barr!

Piou a lavaro biken ar c'hemmesk, an drukbuilh
Hag ar stourm araog mervel en tarziou o tiruilh?
Ouz tammou koat, er gwerniel, en deleou a yud
Em krog gant o ivin evel eur brankad tud.

Oll, o nervennou stegnet, o lagad digor braz,
En eur grena gant anoued, gant terzien ha gant glaz,
E c'hedont sikour na deu... A damm dre damm hep eur,
Ar brankad a rouesa, n'euz gour abarz nemeur!

Eur paotr yaouank a Gleder an doa bet an eurvad
Da c'hellout ouz ar rec'hel gant kalz a boan pignat,
Pa glevaz ouz e c'hervel e vreur bihan e traou,
Hag hen lammet d'e zikour... Beuzet int bet o daou.

Tud keiz, war-nez da lakat o zroad ouz douar Breiz,
Edo neuden o c'haloun o tridal en o c'hreiz,
Ha setu ma sank enno kildent eur roc'h garo:
O mousc'hoarz a zo sklaset gant droukliv ar maro.

C'houeac'h hebken o deuz gallet kavout o zamm buez;
Ouspenn kant a zo choumet er mor doun da c'hourvez,
Ar darnvuia Bretoned! O breudeur, mar gallfemp
Rei eur pok da vihana d'ho tal, d'ho pleo distremp!

Paourkeaz relegou kollet, mar gallfed ho kavout,
Mar gallfed monet hebken hed a hed war ho roud,
Gant pegen braz levenez e vijec'h dastumet!
Gant pegen braz karantez e vijec'h briatet?

*

Hogen ar mor 'n euz lazet ha dalc'het ho korfou,
N'hall, ker krenv ma 'zo eo, laza na derc'hel hoc'h eneou.
Ar feiz a yoa 'n ho kaloun, feiz stard ar Vretoned:
Eur beden war ho tiweuz c'houi a zo tremenet.

Beza e oant kristenien hag oll kristenien vad,
Labourerien Plouezoc'h, Sibiril, Plouescat,
Re Blouzevede, Cleder, Rosko ha Plouenan,
Re Gastel, Treflez, Plougoulm ha re Dreflaouenan.

Marz eo nag en doa fizians en e Vamm euz an neac'h
An den yaouank a gevjod chapeled ouz e vreac'h;
Hag hounnez a yoa ivez eur plac'hik a galon
A skrivaz araog mervel: "Va breur, ped evidon!"

Euz strad o linsel finvuz e c'houlenn an anaon
Eur c'horn-douar benniget, kan Iliz ha vaskaon,
Hag ar mor gant pizoni a zilounk ouz an aot
Korfou blonset gant an traz ha morliv a dioujod.

*

Eur gwall-reuz peuriesa pa zispak e graban,
Pa zailh gant e zremm euzus, ne deu ket e-unan:
An eil tarz-môr a beurc'hra labour an hini kent;
Gant skei, ec'h had an Ankou hirnez, goelvan, skrigndent!

D'ar c'houlz ma tlier tanva bara mad ha dudi
Setu n'euz 'met dienez ha kaon e-barz peb ti,
Ha pegeit eo da badout ho reuz, ho naoun, mamm geaz?
Ar paotr a c'hello gounid 'zo war ho parlen c'hoaz.

Ha te, den koz daoubleget, piou harpo da gozni?
Piou 'glozo da zaoulagad en-berr pe dremeni? –
Eat eo da vuia-karet, plac'hik, eat eo d'anaon! –
Intanvez da zeitek vloaz, gwisk da vantel zu-kaon!

Ar mor epad pell amzer a darzo c'hoaz en aot,
Avel ar meaz en teven pell c'hoaz a zuilho geot,
Ha siouaz pell pell ivez e talc'hint beo envor
Ar gwall-bense tud yaouank ha rann-galoun Arvor.

An daoulagad entanet n'o deuz mui a zaelou,
Ar c'hlemvan a zo torret: e doun ar c'halonou
Ar c'heuz, trouz ebet gantan, en em zilet a-ruz,
A grign kig beo ar gouli dre zindan hag e-kuz.

A bell, me 'gav d'in gwelet an nozvez beilhaden,
Ouz taol, an tamm, boued debret; na grik na mik gan den;
Daou, tri skaon a zo goullo, skanviou ar c'hez anaon,
Ar re vihan na gredont sellet outo gant aon.

145

An oll'zo pleget o fenn; er meaz, eur gaouad c'hlo...
Hag oll ez eont a spered da rec'hel Sant-Malo,
E doare pelerined beteg eur bez santel,
Hag eno sioul, heb tinval, e choumont diskabel.

Ha kredi a reont gwelet even d'ar zadorn noz
An *Hilda* gant mor diroll o tonet a Vro-Zaoz;
Gwelet a reont an dispac'h, ar flastr, an tremenvan,
Hag ar c'horvou a-stribilh abarz koueza dindan.

Hag ar galv, ar youc'haden, an hini diveza,
He c'hlevet a reont skiltruz... Hag an tud koz 'n e za
Trumm da rei sikour... Siouaz! Hag hen divorfila!
Hag en em welet er gear ha diroll da ouela!

Setu aze, Kristenien, stad ho kenvroiz keiz!
M'ho ped, en hano Doue hag hon bro ger a Vreiz,
Na nac'hit ket rei d'ezo skoazell hoc'h aluzenn,
Ha kas 'vit o re varo da Zoue ho pedenn.

Glanmor

Translation The Shipwreck of the *Hilda*

(In memory of the Bretons who lost their lives on the rocks of St. Malo on that terrible Saturday night, November 18).

From England they were coming having done their season and happy, / Some were young, some merely children even: / In the steamer *Hilda* they sang as they returned: / Blessed he who has no need to leave his country.

Between their shirts and skin, the bosses of the crew / in their leather belts carried the gold sovereigns, / That gold whose glint should have become / a sustenance and happiness to many a family.

Because the time of the happy evenings had come / to relax at the fire-side and exchange tales; / And many a youngster shivered as he thought / that soon he would be married to the sweetheart that was waiting for him.

In the middle of darkness as black as hell / The voice of the wind snarls and the sea thunders, / The ship groans amidst the waves: "Never mind! / She has a fine helmsman and we are to the harbour".

But suddenly there's a crack: What is it? What is it? / said a sailor running fast; / The rudder! The rudder's gone!" All are quiet, / A fear grips them and everyone is silent.

The ship is now loose, out of control, to go where it wishes / Where will it go in the fullness of its speed? / From his lookout, the captain who appears calm / Issues a command which is not heard.

Like a shot from a cannon a shout is heard; / "Rocks! Rocks ahead!". At once as the rain is pouring / A terrible knock and chaos, hands are raised in fright, / And a single, lonely, huge shout, in the middle of the tempest!

Who can describe the commotion, the troubles / And the fight for life before succumbing to death in the wild waves / To bits of wood, to the masts, to the screeching sirens / They clung by their finger nails like branches of people.

All, their muscles stiff, eyes open wide / Shivering from cold, from fever and cramp / They watched for the help that never came... And by the hour, / The pieces of wood, cleared 'till hardly a man was left.

A young lad from Cleder managed / With difficulty to climb the rocks / When he heard his younger brother calling him below, / He sprung to his aid – both were drowned.

People, about to set foot on Breton soil, / Their hearts shaking within them, / And behold the teeth of the rocks sinking into them / Their smiles frozen in paleness of death.

Six alone managed to save their lives; / Over a hundred lie in the deep sea, / Most of them Bretons! Brothers, if only I could / But kiss your foreheads and wet hair!

Fossiled lost wretches, if we only could find you, / if only we could trace you, / With such joy as we would raise you! / With such love you would be embraced.

*   *   *

But the sea that killed and kept their bodies, / Cannot, despite its strength, kill nor keep your souls; / The faith that was in your hearts, the strong faith of the Bretons: / One prayer at your end was offered.

They were Christians and all good Christians, / Workers of Plouezoc'h, Sibiril, Plouescat, / Those of Plouzevede, Cleder, Roscoff and Plouenan, / Those of Kastel, Treflez, Plougoulm and Treflaouenan.

Strange if he had no faith in the Mother above / The young man with the rosary on his arm; / and she was a good woman / The one who wrote before dying: "My brother, pray for me!"

In the depths of their uneasy shroud death asked / For a piece of holy ground, a church chant which hides fear, / And the sea miserly vomited onto the beach / Battered bodies with pale faces.

*   *   *

A terrible disaster usually when it unsheaths its claws, / When it comes with its awful face; / The second haze finishes the work of its predecessor; / It strikes, and sows grief and pain!

147

At the time when the good bread and pleasure should have been enjoyed / There is now but grief and despair in every house, / How long will your suffering last, your hunger, dear mother? / The boy who may earn is still in your arms.

And you, hunch-backed old woman, who will keep you in your old age? / Who will shut your eyes when you perish? / Gone is your sweetheart, girl, gone to his death – / Seventeen year old widow, put on your black coat of mourning!

The sea will long break on the beach / The wind will long batter the grass on the dunes / And alas, also, long will the memory live / Of the terrible disaster in the hearts of the people of Arvor.

No tears remain in the bloodshot eyes, / The moaning in the depths of their hearts silenced / The longing, quietly, released / To eat away the living flesh of the pain.

From afar, on the night of the grief I thought I saw, / On the table, a little food had been eaten: no word or movement from anyone; / Two, three empty stools, dear stools of death, / and the little ones afraid to look at them.

All with heads bowed; outside, a shower of rain... / All with their thoughts at the rocks of St. Malo / Like pilgrimages at a holy tomb, / there they stand, silent and bare-headed.

And they believe they see as on that Saturday / The *Hilda* on a fierce sea coming from England; / They see the commotion, the collision, the death, / And the bodies hanging before falling under.

And the shouting, the cry, the last one, / They hear them. The grandfather goes / Immediately to help... Alas! Then he wakes! / Finds himself at home and breaks into tears!

That then, Christians, is the state of your dear countrymen / I pray you, in the name of God and our dear Brittany / Don't refuse them the aid of your charity, / And to their loved ones who died give your prayers to God.

The Johnnies

(This song was recorded on Ile de Batz)

Dans notre métier, ce n'est pas tout rose
Si l'on a les poches pleines de *pognon*
Pour les récolter c'est une autre chose
Faut voir à l'oeuvre le marchand d'oignons
Courant de portes en portes
Chargés comme des *bourricots*

148

En attendant que quelqu'un sorte
Pour alléger notre fardeau
Mais c'est encore.....
Siouaz eun all! chomet a biou.

Et tout le long des rues
s'en va le pauvre Johnnie,
l'air gai, mais l'âme ennuie,
qu'il pleuve, qu'il neige, jour et nuit.
Oui, c'est lui qui *chine*
jusqu'au dernier penny.
C'est le métier de nos Johnnies, à la *chine*
Si par bonheur la chance le favorise.
Il est heureuse comme un poisson dans l'eau
à peine clos, c'est le *bistrot* qu'il vise
pour deguster une bière aussitot.
Redoublant alors de courage,
Il reprend encore son *boulot*
le voila plus gai qui voyage
portant comme un rien son fardeau
confiant la chique à tous ses concurrents
........, *eman echu gantan.*

Quand le dimanche où l'on se repose
Tant que l'on veut dans un lit bien chaud
Elle est bien gagneé, cette courte pause
apres 6 jours de *trimand* au galop
Et aussitôt qu'on nous prepare la soupe
Quelque chose d'appetissant,
on joue à ''coeur, figue et je coupe''
Tremen ar zul, echu gantan.

Translation

In our trade, life isn't all honey / Even if our pockets are full of money / It's another matter to get them so / One must see the onion seller at work / Running from door to door / Laden like an ass / Waiting for someone to come out / To lighten his load / But once again..... / Alas, another! Has been lost.

Along the streets / Goes the poor Johnny / his appearance is light but his spirit is low / Be it rain, or snow, day or night. / Yes, this one haggling / To the last penny. / That's the trade of our Johnny, selling from door to door. / If by good luck fate smiles on him / He is as happy as a fish in water, / Hardly finished, and its for the pub he goes immediately to drink a beer. Then having refreshed his strength / he starts his work again / There he is happier on his journey / carrying his load as if it were nothing / getting ahead of his competition / .... and then he is gone.

Then on Sunday when one rests / and stays as long as one wishes in a warm bed / He deserves it, this short break / after six days of slogging. / And then the soup is prepared for us / something to raise the appetite, / play our card game. / Thus the Sunday is spent, and then he is gone.